Skye Fargo cursed himself for a fool.

He let himself be distracted by Virginia Ragsdale when the rancher's redheaded daughter asked him into her room. He didn't see the door swing open until the two Mexicans were inside with their guns cocked and leveled. He didn't have to ask who they were—Santiago Maxwell's men.

Fargo tried to ease his Colt from his holster. But the gunmen were watching him like twin hawks. He had no choice. He set it down on the floor and held his hands out from his sides. "What's this all about?" he demanded. "What does Santiago want with Miss Ragsdale?"

Without warning, the Mexican in the red sash lashed the barrel of his gun across Fargo's temple.

"It is not the woman Santiago wants," Red Sash hissed. "He sent us to deal with the *bastardo* who killed Pedro Valdez and Jose Gonzalez."

Red Sash shook Fargo, then tossed him down. Fargo tried to marshal his thoughts, but his head was spinning.

All he could hear were the snarling words: "Time to die, *gringo*."

THE
TRAILSMAN
169

SOCORRO
SLAUGHTER

by

Jon Sharpe

A SIGNET BOOK

SIGNET
Published by the Penguin Group
Penguin Books USA Inc., 375 Hudson Street,
New York, New York 10014, U.S.A.
Penguin Books Ltd, 27 Wrights Lane,
London W8 5TZ, England
Penguin Books Australia Ltd, Ringwood,
Victoria, Australia
Penguin Books Canada Ltd, 10 Alcorn Avenue,
Toronto, Ontario, Canada M4V 3B2
Penguin Books (N.Z.) Ltd, 182–190 Wairau Road,
Auckland 10, New Zealand

Penguin Books Ltd, Registered Offices:
Harmondsworth, Middlesex, England

First published by Signet, an imprint of Dutton Signet,
a division of Penguin Books USA Inc.

First Printing, January, 1996
10 9 8 7 6 5 4 3 2 1

The first chapter of this book originally appeared in *Kiowa Command*,
the one hundred sixty-eighth volume in this series.

  REGISTERED TRADEMARK—MARCA REGISTRADA

Printed in the United States of America

The Trailsman

Beginnings . . . they bend the tree and they mark the man. Skye Fargo was born when he was eighteen. Terror was his midwife, vengeance his first cry. Killing spawned Skye Fargo, ruthless, cold-blooded murder. Out of the acrid smoke of gunpowder still hanging in the air, he rose, cried out a promise never forgotten.

The Trailsman they began to call him all across the West: searcher, scout, hunter, the man who could see where others only looked, his skills for hire but not his soul, the man who lived each day to the fullest, yet trailed each tomorrow. Skye Fargo, the Trailsman, the seeker who could take the wildness of a land and the wanting of a woman and make them his own.

1860, New Mexico Territory—
Where hatred had spawned a killing ground . . .

1

When a man has ridden a horse day after day, month after month, he gets to know that animal as well as he knows himself.

Skye Fargo was no exception. Like many a horseman, he thought of his Ovaro more as a companion than a simple beast of burden. He knew its moods, knew the limits to which he could push the pinto stallion without running it into the ground. He knew how it would react in any given situation. He also knew the many sounds it made and what each sound meant.

So when the horse gave out with a low, rumbling nicker in the middle of the night, Skye Fargo was instantly awake, his hand on the Colt strapped to his right hip. He gave a single shake of his head to clear lingering cobwebs, then strained his senses to learn why the Ovaro was agitated.

The answer became clear moments later when the crisp breeze carried a faint crunch to Fargo's ears, just such a noise as a foot stepping on gravel might make.

Fargo rolled onto his left side and pushed into a crouch, facing southwest, the direction the sound came from. Earlier that night he'd made camp in a chaparral which bordered the narrow dusty road from Albuquerque to Las Cruces, a normal precaution in a territory plagued by Apache and Navaho marauders. He'd figured that he was so well hidden, no one else could find him.

Evidently he had been mistaken.

Fargo removed his hat and leaned it against his saddle, which he had been using as a pillow. Then, after hiking his blanket high enough to give the impression there was someone under it, he crept into the dark and hunkered behind a cluster of mesquite.

The telltale jingle of spurs told Fargo his visitors weren't Indians, since no self-respecting warrior would be caught dead in them. His lake blue eyes narrowed when he saw a shadow detach itself from a bush several dozen yards away and move toward the stallion. There was something about the shadow which bothered him. It was on all fours, low to the ground as a slinking man would be, but it moved too quickly, too smoothly to be human.

Then it hit him. The creature was a dog, not a man. Now Fargo understood how his camp has been discovered; the dog had picked up the Ovaro's scent.

Fargo held himself as still as the mesquite, his thumb on the hammer of the pistol. Behind the dog other shapes had appeared, three of them moving quietly forward, their features shrouded by *sombreros*. Moonlight glittered dully off six-shooters.

Bandidos, Fargo reasoned. Back in Albuquerque he'd heard tell that a band of bandits was making life miserable for folks living in the vicinity of Socorro. These men might be part of that band.

The dog proved to be well trained. It advanced to within a few yards of the small clearing and paused to sniff. The stallion watched closely with head held high and ears pricked, but the dog paid it no attention. All the dog seemed interested in was the blanket.

Fargo saw one of the figures glide up close to the mongrel. At a whispered word, the dog stalked toward the saddle. Body bent lower than ever, lips pulled back to reveal tapered teeth, it moved a few feet, froze for several seconds, then moved a little farther.

The stallion stamped a front hoof, causing the dog to swivel around. It appeared about to attack but a sharp gesture by the figure sent it on its way again.

Slowly raising the Colt, Fargo took deliberate aim at the dog's head. The animal was more dangerous than the bandits and had to be taken care of first. He started to ease back the hammer slowly so the click would not be all that loud.

To Fargo's chagrin, the dog heard. It immediately whirled toward the mesquite and growled. Fargo shifted the pistol slightly to compensate and squeezed the trigger, but just as he did the beast lunged to the left and streaked into the chaparral.

At the retort, all hell broke loose. The Ovaro reared and whinnied shrilly while the three bandits cut loose, their revolvers spitting flame and smoke, the night rocking to the thunder of gun blasts.

Lead clipped limbs and smacked into the ground on both sides of Fargo as he threw himself to the left and rolled. Through a gap he spied one of the trio. Banging off a pair of swift shots, he rose onto his right knee and was about to rush deeper into the mesquite to outflank the cutthroats when a lightning form hurtled out of nowhere and caught him flush on the shoulder.

The impact bowled Fargo over. He nearly cried out when razor teeth sheared through his buckskin shirt into his flesh, drawing a spurt of blood. Flat on his back, he lashed out, clubbing the dog across the skull as it let go of his shoulder and snapped at his neck. The blow staggered the animal long enough for Fargo to scramble backward, out of reach of those deadly fangs.

Or so he thought.

Fargo snapped the Colt high to put a slug into the mongrel, yet as fast as he was, the dog was faster. It pounced, those iron jaws clamping shut on his wrist. Waves of pain coursed up his arm. His instinctive reaction was to jerk his arm loose but he knew that in doing so he would shred his own wrist, so he kicked the dog instead. His boot heel slammed into the brute's front legs so hard they were knocked out from under it.

The beast let go. Fargo pivoted and trained the barrel on its temple. He would have fired had not one of the bandits hurtled out of the brush. A six-gun roared and Fargo answered in kind. The *bandido* stumbled, cursed in Spanish, then fell.

Fargo again went to slay the dog but it had more lives than a cat and was on him before he could squeeze the trigger. This time it came straight for his jugular, snarling and bristling in bestial rage. Without thinking, he shoved his gun under the animal's lower jaw and held it briefly at bay while scrabbling to the left.

The dog went into a frenzy. It bit and tore at Fargo, tearing his sleeve wide open and ripping into his skin. He battered it with his other arm and continued to kick, but the rain of blows had no effect.

Keenly aware that the third bandit might show up at any moment, Fargo coiled both legs and drove them into the mongrel's belly. The dog went flying, recovered in a heartbeat, and, undaunted, sprang once more.

This time Fargo was ready. He fanned the Colt, three shots so closely spaced they sounded like one. It was as if an invisible hammer smashed into the dog, catapulting it head over heels into the nearest bush.

Fargo gained his feet and crouched, waiting for the last bandit to appear. He quickly reloaded.

The dog twitched and growled and tried to stand but couldn't. Defiant to the last, it snarled at him before sinking limply to the arid soil.

A minute went by, then several more. All Fargo heard was the wind rustling the mesquite and the nervous prancing of the stallion. He straightened when a distant drumming of hoofs revealed the last *bandido* had had enough and was headed for parts unknown. Lowering the Colt, he breathed in deeply to calm his racing pulse.

Before Fargo could take stock of his wounds, he had to check the others. The dog didn't move when he nudged it. Pressing his hand to its neck, he confirmed the beast was dead. The same held true for the second bandit.

Veering to the clearing, Fargo found the first *bandido* lying facedown in a spreading inky pool. Fargo kicked the man's pistol out of reach, then knelt and placed his hand on the killer's shoulder.

Groaning loudly, the bandit opened his eyes. He was swarthy, his chin covered with stubble, his mustache slick with grease. Blood trickled from the corners of his mouth when he tried to speak and a fit of coughing racked him. Finally, he sputtered *"Diablo?"*

Making a guess, Fargo answered, "The dog is dead."

The *bandido* sighed. "That is too bad, gringo. *Diablo* was a good *perro*. He served me well." The man bit his lower lip for a short while. "Before I go, I would like to know who you are."

Fargo offered no reply.

"Is it so much for a man to ask?" the bandit asked weakly. "What is wrong with wanting to know the name of the *hombre* who has done what so many others were not able to do? Because of you, I will soon be burning in the eternal fire. The least you can do is tell me."

Wary of a trick, Fargo bent down and did as the killer wanted.

"Gracias. I am Pedro Valdez. Let others know, *por favor.* I want word to get back to my parents in Chihuahua. They are the only ones who will give a damn." More coughing caused the bandit to quake and moan.

Fargo checked for hidden weapons and discovered a dagger in Valdez's boot and a derringer wedged under the cutthroat's wide brown leather belt. "Were you waiting for me to turn my back?"

Valdez mustered a wan grin. "A man can always hope, senor." He inhaled raggedly. "You are a tough one. I can see that. But there is one who is tougher. Stay in this country awhile and Santiago will pay you back for what you have done this night. Yes, *hombre.* Santiago will——."

The words trailed off. Pedro Valdez uttered a long sigh which ended in a strangled gasp.

Fargo stepped to the saddle and shrugged out of his shirt. The dog had done slight damage to his wrist but his shoulder was another matter. A two-inch gash, half as deep, still bled freely. He had to cauterize it before the loss of blood weakened him.

Using the pile of kindling he had gathered before turning in, Fargo soon had his small campfire rekindled. From his right boot he took the Arkansas toothpick he favored and heated the slender blade in the dancing flames. Soon the knife was hot enough. He stuffed part of his shirt into his mouth, clamped down, and then applied the blade to the gash.

There was a loud sizzling. Searing agony lanced through the Trailsman. The acrid scent of burnt flesh filled his nostrils, and for a couple of seconds the stars spun crazily. He bowed his head until the sickening sensation passed.

Running his fingers over the wound, Fargo confirmed that the knife had done its job. The bleeding had indeed stopped. Now he only had to worry about infection setting in.

After sliding the toothpick into its ankle sheath, Fargo dressed, sat on the blanket, and awaited the dawn. Sleep was out of the question. As a precaution, he took his heavy-caliber Sharps from the saddle scabbard and rested the rifle across his legs.

In ten days Fargo had to be in Las Cruces. Much closer, only a few hours to the south, was Socorro. He would have plenty of time to stop there for a spell and let his wound mend some before he pushed on.

Traveling in a weakened state in the territory of New Mexico wasn't advisable. The land was as hard as flint, as merciless as a Mescalero on the warpath. The most simple of mistakes could well prove deadly, which was why scores of pilgrims lost their lives every year. A single moment's carelessness was all it took.

Fargo had learned the hard way not to take the land or its people for granted. When on the go, he made it a habit to check his back trail frequently. When camping, he picked out-of-the-way places and kept his fires small, as would an Indian. When in the desert, he knew how to find water where most whites had no idea it would be. In the mountains he could find game without half trying.

So although Fargo had been wounded, he wasn't worried. He didn't do as many greenhorns would have done, panic. Keeping his wits was another important trait experience had taught him.

The man who lost his head was more apt to lose his life.

Sunrise was an hour off when Fargo made a pot of coffee

14

and downed two cups of the piping hot brew. As pink-and-yellow bands streaked the eastern horizon, he rose and went in search of the mounts belonging to the slain bandits. He half hoped the animals had run off so he wouldn't need to tote the corpses into Socorro, but as luck would have it he located a bay and a sorrel hidden in the chaparral about two hundred yards from the clearing. Neither shied when he grabbed their reins and led them back.

A golden crown framed the skyline when Fargo stepped into the stirrups and wound his way through the chaparral to the road. Pointing the stallion due south, he rode at a trot for the first mile to put some distance between himself and the clearing in case the *bandido* who got away returned with friends.

Presently four riders appeared, heading north. They were cowhands, though, and they gave Fargo a wide berth when they spotted the bodies. So did the driver of a buckboard, half an hour later. The man cracked his whip to spur the team on while the elderly woman beside him covered the lower portion of her face with a red shawl and gawked at the bodies through eyes the size of walnuts.

It wasn't long afterward that Socorro came into sight, its many long, low buildings close to the Rio Grande, which glistened to the east.

Fargo looked neither right nor left as he entered the town and rode down the middle of the main street. Still, there was no mistaking the sensation he created. Many passersby halted to study the bodies. Men fingered rifles or pistols. Women grasped small children and made them look away. Several dogs added to the commotion by darting out of a side street and yipping like loco coyotes.

In front of a saloon Fargo drew rein. He looped the reins to all three horses around the hitch rail, swiped dust from his buckskins, and sauntered into the cool, gloomy interior.

"What's your poison, stranger?" the beanpole barkeep asked.

"A bottle of the best tonsil varnish you've got," Fargo declared, striding to the bar and slapping enough coins to cover the cost onto the counter.

15

The bartender eyed Fargo's torn shoulder and sleeve, his brow knit. "Looks to me as if you've earned the treat. Had a lick of trouble, did you?"

"Does the name Pedro Valdez mean anything to you?"

It was an innocent question on Fargo's part. He started to reach for the bottle but the barkeep went rigid in the act of handing it over. So did everyone else in the saloon, and the place became as silent as a tomb. Fargo scanned the room, then chuckled. "From the look of things, Valdez must be one popular fella."

"Are you joshing, mister?" the bartender said. "Valdez is the second most wanted man in all of New Mexico. He's a born killer from south of the border who joined up with the Maxwell gang a while back. There's no telling how many innocent people he's butchered. Why, if he was to walk in here right this minute, I'd throttle him with my bare hands."

Fargo got hold of the bottle and opened it. "Be my guest, friend."

"How's that?"

"Valdez is right outside. You're welcome to go out and strangle the daylights out of him if you want." Fargo tipped the whiskey and drank greedily, feeling the liquid scorch a path down his throat, washing away the dust of the trail. He ignored the mass exodus as the customers flocked to the batwing doors. By the time they straggled back inside he had a third of the bottle polished off and a warm glow in the pit of his stomach.

In the lead was the bartender. "I don't believe it, stranger! You made wolf meat of Pedro Valdez!"

Fargo set down the bottle and smacked his lips. "It's a habit of mine when someone is trying to kill me."

"I'm Joe O'Keefe," the man said while moving behind the bar. "A cousin of mine was cut to ribbons by the Maxwell gang four months ago, along with the pretty filly he was fixing to marry." His voice choked with emotion. "I was real fond of young Ed. He was going to go to the law school back East to make something of himself." O'Keefe pushed the coins toward

Fargo. "So you can keep your money. That bottle is on the house, and anything else you want, to boot."

Suddenly Fargo was surrounded by beaming citizens of Socorro who clapped him on the back and thanked him over and over. Their gratitude was genuine but it made Fargo feel uncomfortable. Killing Valdez had been a sheer fluke, the result of being in the wrong place at the wrong time. He didn't feel right being made out to be some kind of hero.

"It's too bad the marshal is off delivering a prisoner up to Santa Fe," O'Keefe remarked. "Otherwise he'd be in here buying you all the drinks you could down. He's been after Valdez for months now but never saw hide nor hair of the vermin."

"Who can blame him?" a patron said. "Maxwell was raised in this part of the country and knows it better than anyone. There ain't a man alive who can track him to his lair."

O'Keefe, partly in jest, addressed Fargo. "Maybe you'd like to try, mister. Put windows in that buzzard's skull and you'll be the toast of the whole territory. Hell, we'd vote you in as governor in a landslide."

"I'm just passing through."

From the front of the saloon a deep voice boomed. "That's a crying shame, mister. Maybe five thousand dollars will get you to change your mind."

Another hush fell over the room as all eyes swiveled toward the speaker, a beefy man who packed more corded muscle on his stout frame than most five men combined. It showed in the rippling layers on his neck and huge hands as he bulled his way through the ring of admirers to confront Fargo. His face was seamed with wrinkles and had been bronzed by long exposure to the sun. His clothes and wide-brimmed hat marked him as a man of means, a rancher, perhaps, judging by the large calluses Fargo felt when they shook hands.

"William Ragsdale is my handle, and I own the Bar R, just about the biggest spread this side of the Rio Grande. Who might you be?"

"Skye Fargo."

Ragsdale blinked and stepped back to give Fargo a closer

17

scrutiny. "That name is familiar for some reason. Do I know you from somewhere?"

"It's a small world."

Crooking an elbow, the rancher leaned on the counter. "I reckon. So what do you say to the five thousand?"

The notion of earning so much money was tantalizing. Fargo was like most men and enjoyed living high on the hog on occasion. Games of high stakes poker, nights spent in the company of willing doves, and eating at classy restaurants were some of his favorite pastimes, but they did not come cheap. He was tempted until he thought of his appointment in Las Cruces. It was bound to take longer than a week and a half to track Maxwell down.

William Ragsdale took the pause as an encouraging sign. "Ask any man here. I'm as good as my word. If you kill Maxwell, I'll have the cash in your hand before the body is cold."

"If you want him planted so badly, why not round up a bunch of your hands and do it yourself?"

Someone coughed nervously but the rancher didn't take offense. "Do you think I haven't tried? Fifteen, twenty times, at least. He's struck my ranch more often than I care to count, bushwacking my punchers or slaughtering cattle for the sheer hell of it. Each time he got away as slick as could be."

"He's bound to slip up sooner or later," Fargo said, and swallowed more rotgut.

The rancher snorted. "I can see that you don't know what we're dealing with here. Santiago Maxwell is a half-breed. His pa was a breed himself, part Mexican, part Navaho. His ma was white trash. Think about that mix a minute. To make things worse, he lived with the tribe for a few years when he was younger, and he learned all their heathen ways. There isn't a white man alive who can match him in the wild." Ragsdale paused. "But something tells me you could."

"I have business elsewhere," Fargo explained. He would have gone on but for a most aromatic fragrance which seemed to fill the room all at once. Turning, he beheld the source, a redheaded vision of loveliness in a tight riding outfit who was striding boldly toward them.

"Pa, I'm tired of waiting out in that awful sun. How much longer are you going to be?"

The customers parted to let her through, every man there doffing his hat in respect, a few averting their eyes as if afraid to gaze at her.

The vision was heedless of them all. She was in her early twenties with a complexion as smooth as glass and an hour-glass figure most woman would die for. Her eyes were sparkling blue, her lips the color of ripe cherries.

"Virginia!" Ragsdale barked. "A proper lady doesn't enter saloons! Go outside and wait until I'm done. I'm trying to persuade this gentleman to go after Maxwell for us."

Grinning impishly, the daughter regarded Fargo a few moments, then draped her slim hands on her shapely hips. "I do so hope you will agree, mister. We haven't had a prime specimen like you in these parts in ages."

Ragsdale flushed scarlet. "That will be quite enough! Outside with you this instant!"

Fargo felt a familiar tightness in his throat as he watched Virginia sashay from the premises, her supple bottom swaying in a frank invitation.

"I apologize for her behavior," Ragsdale was saying. "She's always been too headstrong for her own good." He cleared his throat in embarrassment. "Now how about my offer? Are you willing to ride out to the Bar R sometime soon and hear me out?"

Before Skye Fargo quite knew what he was doing, his mouth moved of its own accord. "Why not? I planned on staying here a few days anyway, so I guess it can't hurt." He raised the bottle and noticed his reflection in the mirror, but in his mind's eye all he saw were Virginia Ragsdale's delicious curves. The scent of her perfume hung in the air, promising treasure beyond compare.

"Excellent! You won't regret your decision."

"I hope not," Fargo said, and he had never meant anything more.

2

There are hangovers, and then there are *hangovers*.

Skye Fargo was dimly aware of a gnawing ache in the back of his head as he slowly came back to life. A horrible, gut-wrenching knot in the pit of his stomach warned him not to eat anything for a few hours. He moved his tongue, which felt as thick as a woolly caterpillar and just as hairy, then opened his eyes. And promptly wished he hadn't. Brilliant sunlight streamed in the lone window, the glare so painful he had to squint to see.

"What was I thinking of?" Fargo mumbled to himself. Rising onto his elbows, he looked around, trying to recollect where he was and how he had gotten there.

Fargo figured that he was in a hotel room. The bed, the two chairs, the washbasin, and furnishings were like countless others he had seen, except in one respect. They were all the highest quality, from the plush mattress on which he had passed out to the silver basin to the expensive lace curtains. It had to be the best hotel in all of Socorro, and he couldn't imagine what had possessed him to take a room there when he was so low on funds.

"I must be the biggest idiot who ever lived," Fargo grumbled while swinging his feet onto the carpeted floor.

"If you say so, handsome."

Startled, Fargo swung around, his hand automatically dropping to his Colt. He was flabbergasted to see Virginia Ragsdale in a chair in the corner. Her hair had been done up and she wore a striking green dress which highlighted the sensuous curves of her body in all the right places. Bathed as she was by the sunshine, she presented an incredible picture of raw beauty, as ravishing a woman as he had ever set eyes on. A lump of pure desire formed in his throat and he swallowed, hard.

The redhead acted amused by his befuddled state. "I do declare! It lives! It breathes! I was beginning to think you'd sleep the whole day through."

"Where am I?" Fargo blurted, struggling to snap out of the lethargy which gripped him. For the life of him he couldn't remember a thing other than a near endless round of drinks paraded before him by the grateful people of Socorro. He seemed to recall visiting eight or nine saloons and being treated royally in every one. From then on, everything was a blur.

"You don't know?" Virginia said, and laughed lightly. "Why, you're in room 207 at the Excelsior. Some of your drinking *compadres* brought you here about four in the morning."

Drinking *compadres?* Fargo couldn't remember a single one. The night had been a steady stream of smiling faces, each no different from the other.

"My pa paid for this room on your behalf," Virginia revealed. "And I had Barton keep an eye on you. He told your friends where to bring you after you keeled over."

"Barton?"

"The man my pa hired a while back to watch over me. He's outside the door right this minute, making sure we're not disturbed."

Fargo had a few answers but there were still points he was unclear on. "What are you still doing here? I thought you left last night with your father."

That smile of hers was positively devilish. "Haven't you heard? It's a woman's prerogative to change her mind whenever she wants." She leaned forward as if confiding a secret. "I was in no hurry to get back to the Bar R. It's so boring there, with so little to do. You gave me the perfect excuse to stay over another night."

"I did?" Fargo said, standing. He had to grit his teeth when his stomach tried to claw its way up his throat.

"Sure. For some reason my pa is convinced you're the man

who can end all our woes. He doesn't want you to slip off without seeing him first. So it was easy for me to talk him into letting me escort you out to the ranch."

Fargo shuffled to the basin, removed his hat, and dipped his face in the cool water. It felt glorious. He held his breath as long as he could, then straightened and stared at the pitiful excuse for a human being reflected in the mirror. He truly looked just like death warmed over.

Virginia had stood. "My goodness. I feared you were going to drown yourself," she quipped. "I suppose you'll want to pull yourself together before we head for the Bar R. I'm in room 208. If you'd like to eat before we go, fetch me. I know a nice restaurant a few blocks from here."

Food was the last thing Fargo wanted. He had a half mind to refuse to go with her, but he had told her father he would hear the man out and he had to abide by his word. Turning as she walked to the door, he said, "I could use some coffee. I'll meet you in the lobby in about fifteen minutes."

"I'll be waiting," Virginia said in a husky tone.

Fargo went over and gripped the latch. "Allow me." He opened the door to be polite and promptly tensed on beholding the man who lounged against the opposite wall.

The bodyguard was a tall drink of water dressed in black, including a black vest decorated with silver studs. From around his waist hung a matched pair of nickel-plated Colts sporting ivory grips. He had a thin, sallow face and a waxed mustache no thicker than the point of a pencil. His dark eyes were oddly flat, like those of a rattler, and he gazed at Fargo much as a wolf might gaze at intended prey.

"Mr. Fargo, I'd like you to meet Cole Barton," Virginia said. "He's from Texas, where I understand he earned quite a reputation as a gun shark."

"Howdy," the gunman said with no particular warmth.

Fargo merely nodded. He had an instinctive dislike for the man, the result of having run into hardcase leather slappers like Barton many times before. They were cut from the same rough cloth; cold, callous, and much too eager to kill for the mere sake of killing.

Virginia reached up and touched a finger to Fargo's chin. "Fifteen minutes, big man. Don't keep me waiting." She flounced out and her watchdog dutifully swaggered in her wake, his thumbs hooked in his gunbelt.

Fargo closed the door and went to the basin to make himself presentable. He couldn't fault Ragsdale for hiring a man like the Texan, not if the situation around Socorro was half as bad as everyone made it out to be. Based on the few snatches of conversation he could recall from the night before, it was plain the townsfolk were at their wits' end.

Santiago Maxwell had become the scourge of the territory. For over a year he had been raiding at will, slaying scores of people and plundering to his heart's content. Many of those killed by his gang were tortured before they died, their bodies so badly mutilated it was difficult for their loved ones to identify them.

A demon like Maxwell had to be stopped. The marshal had tried time and again, the local ranchers had banded together and tried, bounty hunters had tried, and all had failed.

Fargo could appreciate the town's plight. Already a few families had left rather than stay and invite tragedy. If Maxwell continued to ravage the countryside, more and more would depart with each passing month. If the tide went unchecked, eventually Sorocco would shrivel up and die and the outlying ranchers would be forced into ruin. It was a bleak prospect.

Presently, wearing a spare shirt, Fargo ventured downstairs. Virginia Ragsdale and the Texan were over by the entrance. He joined them, admiring the cleavage her dress displayed and the enticing outline of her thighs.

"Mercy, you look like a whole new man," the redhead teased. She offered her arm, and when he took it, guided him out onto the hot, dusty street.

The heat and dazzling brightness hit Fargo like a physical blow, making him wince. Glancing skyward, he learned it was well past noon. Few people were abroad. Horses stood with heads hung low at hitch rails while the town dogs slumbered in handy patches of shade.

"This way," Virginia said, leading off. She pressed her side against his and squeezed his arm. "What marvelous biceps you have, Skye. I bet that you're one of the few who could hold his own against my pa."

"Tough, is he?"

"You don't know the half of it. He's never been beaten, not by another man, not by drought or flood or anything," Virginia declared proudly.

"Except Santiago Maxwell."

A cloud came over Virginia's ravishing features. "True. Except him. But unlike most of the folks hereabouts, my pa hasn't given up. He believes we can stop Maxwell. All we need is a little bit of luck and the right man." Her hip brushed his. "Namely you."

"Don't get your hopes up," Fargo advised. "I haven't agreed to go after Maxwell yet."

"You will," Virginia responded smugly.

Fargo didn't bother arguing. Time would tell. As things stood, it would take a heap of convincing to get him to delay his trip to Las Cruces. To change the subject, he said, "Who put my saddlebags and other gear in my room?"

Virginia jerked a thumb over her shoulder. Fifteen yards behind them strolled Cole Barton. "I had him handle your plunder. Your horse is over to the livery."

"I'm obliged," Fargo said. He was also annoyed at himself. It was a serious breach of common sense for him to get so booze blind that he forgot to tend to the Ovaro. In the West a man's horse was as essential to surviving as breath itself, and had to be treated accordingly.

"Think nothing of it," Virginia said. "I was just being neighborly, like the Good Book says to do."

Fargo grinned at her sly wink. She was a brazen one, that was for sure, and he knew that if he played his cards right he was in for a real treat. The prospect made his mouth water. Which was more than could be said for the odor of cooking food which assailed him as he entered the restaurant. Right away his stomach started flipping and flopping like a fish out of water. It must have shown, because the redhead tittered on glancing at his face.

"You're not going to be sick, are you?"

"I sure as hell hope not." Fargo pulled out a chair for her, then sat, grateful to be off his feet. He saw a waitress carrying a heaped plate of beef and potatoes to a nearby table and shifted so he couldn't see the customer eat.

Virginia was enjoying herself immensely. Chuckling, she ordered coffee for both of them and instructed the waitress to keep his cup filled until he had enough.

Barton took a table across the room and sat so he could observe them and the door. He slid his chair back a foot or so in order to be able to unlimber his hardware while seated without being impaired.

"That gent knows his business," Fargo mentioned.

"The word is that he's sent fourteen men to boot hill at one time or another," Virginia said. "Four of them he killed in a single gunfight down in San Antonio. They say he shot all four before one could clear leather. Mexicans, they were."

Fargo wondered why that should be significant. Dead was dead, whether a person was white, Mexican, or an Indian. He sipped his coffee and forgot about the remark.

Virginia propped her chin on her hands and stared closely at him. "So tell me. Is there a little lady tucked away somewhere? With five or six brats underfoot, maybe?"

"No."

"What a shame," Virginia said, her eyes belying her statement. "How is it that a good-looking fellow like you hasn't been roped and branded yet?"

"I fight shy of branding irons," Fargo said, "or irons of any kind." He let the matter drop since he wasn't about to justify his personal life to her or anyone else. About to lift his cup again, he happened to see Barton glance through the huge window and stiffen ever so slightly. A moment later the bell over the door tinkled and into the restaurant strode a pair of men.

Both were Mexicans. Both wore sombreros and pistols slung low. One had a red sash from which jutted the bejeweled

25

hilt of a large knife. They moved to a table in front of the window.

None of the other customers acted the least bit concerned. As well they shouldn't, since there were as many if not more residents of Mexican descent in Socorro than there were whites. This stemmed from the fact that until a decade ago New Mexico had been part of Mexico itself.

All of which made Fargo more puzzled by Cole Barton's behavior. The gunman had not taken his eyes off the pair once and had lowered his hands to his lap, within easy reach of those fancy pistols. If the Mexicans noticed, they didn't show it.

The waitress had returned and Virginia Ragsdale was ordering steak. "Are you sure that you wouldn't like a bite to eat before we leave?" she asked him. "It's a long ride to the plains of San Augustin."

"Is that where the ranch is?"

"More or less. We own land from Horse Springs clear into the San Mateo Mountains. My parents settled there over forty years ago when it was nothing but wilderness overrun with savages. Pa drove them off and brought in a small herd. Now, we own the biggest ranch in these parts and have more cattle than anyone in New Mexico."

"How many hands do you have working for you?"

"It varies. About forty at any given time."

Fargo whistled. A spread could be judged by the size of its outfit. Clearly the ranch was everything the father and daughter claimed. It struck him as strange that Santiago Maxwell had seen fit to raid the Bar R. Usually bandits left the bigger spreads alone.

The matronly waitress hovered over them, her pencil poised over her pad. "About ordering?" she impatiently prompted.

"Sorry," Fargo said. His stomach had settled down enough that the thought of food no longer made him queasy. He decided to take a gamble. "Bring me a small steak and toast."

For the next ten minutes Fargo listened to Virginia tell of her childhood. He learned that she had a passion for the costly things in life, and established that she had an independent streak as wide as the Rio Grande. She got around to talking about her folks and mentioned in an offhand manner that they were having a hard time because of her sister.

"Does she cause a lot of trouble?" Fargo idly asked.

"If you only knew," Virginia said, not sounding very happy about it. "Jennifer is two years younger than I am. She wasn't allowed to come into town this trip since she's been so naughty lately."

"What did she do?"

Virginia hesitated, and it was then their meals arrived. She ate heartily, saying little until they were done and Fargo had pushed his plate back and reached into a pocket. "There's no need to pay. Darcy will put it on the Bar R's tab."

Fargo shrugged. If they wanted to cater to his needs, that was their affair. He was under no obligation to stay and help out. "When do we ride out?"

"Within the hour, if you want. I have to change and collect my clothes from the Excelsior."

The Mexicans were still at their table, dawdling over burritos and beans. Neither so much as looked in Virginia's direction. Once outside, Fargo hooked elbows with her and politely doffed his hat to a flock of prim and proper biddies who peered down their narrow noses and hardly said two words when Virginia greeted them by name.

"I reckon I'm scandalized," the redhead said in mock dismay after the women were out of earshot. "But it won't be the first time, or the last. Why, if not for my escapades, the upstanding ladies of Socorro would have nothing to gossip about."

They were halfway to the hotel when Fargo checked over a shoulder and saw no sign of Cole Barton. "Where's your nursemaid?"

Virginia looked. "I don't know, but you can rest assured he is close by. He's under strict orders not to let me out of his sight, and he knows Pa would skin him alive if he disobeys."

Fargo hoped his luck held and the bodyguard failed to appear before they reached their rooms. As they crossed the lobby he kept one eye on the door. On the way up the stairs he

27

deliberately crowded Virginia, stepping in so close behind her that their bodies rubbed against one another. She drew up short and turned, a suggestive gleam in her eyes.

"My, you are clumsy all of a sudden."

"It's the whiskey I drank last night," Fargo fibbed, pleased that she made no attempt to go on.

"Barton told me you downed enough to put ten men under the table," Virginia said. "He claims you must be part sieve." She glanced both ways to insure they were alone, then leaned closer, placing her lips a whisker's width from his. "Do you kiss as good as you drink?"

"Better."

"Prove it."

Fargo did. Wrapping his arms around her, he pulled her close. Her full bosom pressed against his chest as her mouth did the same to his lips. Hers parted to admit his tongue and he probed deep, savoring the silken sensation. She purred as might a contented cat, her long nails digging lightly into his back. His manhood surged. Molding his thighs to hers, he forced her back into the wall and cupped her right breast.

Suddenly Virginia broke the kiss and pushed him back. "Dear Lord!" she husked. "You work fast!" She took several breaths to compose herself. "But this isn't the right place to get carried away. Should someone see us and my pa hear of it, there would be hell to pay. There are limits to how much he'll let me get away with."

"It's your loss," Fargo taunted.

Virginia grabbed his hand and hastened to the second floor. She practically flew to her room, inserted the key, and hauled him in after her. Kicking the door shut, she rested her palms on his broad shoulders and snickered. "Now where were we?"

Words were unnecessary. Fargo grasped her buttocks and nibbled on her earlobe. She arched her back, then playfully bit his cheek.

"Like it rough, do you?" Fargo growled. Swooping his hands to her breasts, he mashed them under his fingers and felt her quiver with delight. His lips traced a path from her neck to the top of her heaving mounds.

"Ohhhhhh, I knew you'd be a hellion," Virginia said.

Fargo lathered her breasts while kneading her bottom. She closed her eyes and let out a long sigh, her lower lip quivering. When he slid a hand between her legs and stroked her inner thighs, she cried out softly and tossed her head as if having a fit.

Looping his arms around her waist, Fargo hoisted her off the floor and carried her toward the bed. Virginia ran her hands through his hair, knocking his hat to the floor. She lay back, her hair forming a red halo which accented the lust lining her face.

"I guess we can always leave for the ranch in the morning."

Raising a knee onto the spread, Fargo went to lower himself beside her. He paused. "What about Barton? I don't want to be interrupted."

"Don't fret. He wouldn't dare enter without knocking first. I'll shoo him off if he does."

"He's bound to figure out what we're up to. What if he tells your father?"

Virginia took hold of his shirt. "He's going to admit to letting me out of his sight long enough for us to make love? Somehow, I doubt he's that stupid."

Satisfied, Fargo eased onto his right side. They were nose to nose, chest to breasts. Their mouths joined and they drank greedily of one another. Fargo started to unfasten her dress, then stopped, unsure whether he had heard a metallic rasp behind him. The creak of a floorboard confirmed that he had. Sitting up, he swung around, ready to give the Texan a tongue-lashing, or worse.

Only it wasn't Cole Barton.

The two Mexicans from the restaurant had slipped into the room and closed the door behind them. Their revolvers were leveled and cocked. Nearest to the bed was the man in the red sash, who wagged his six-shooter and snapped in a clipped accent, "Be so good as to shuck your *pistola*, senor, or will I shoot the pretty senorita between the eyes."

Virginia resembled a board. "Do as he says, Skye," she whispered in fear. "They must be two of Maxwell's bunch."

"That we are, senorita," the man wearing the sash stated. "He told us to give you his fondest regards if we had the chance."

Fargo was slowly easing the Colt from its holster. The gunmen were watching him like twin hawks, preventing him from bringing the pistol into play. Setting it down on the floor, he held his hands out from his sides to show he was going to do as they wanted. "What's this all about?" he demanded. "What does Santiago Maxwell have to do with Miss Ragsdale?"

Without warning, the man in the sash stepped forward and lashed the barrel of his gun across Fargo's temple. Fargo had no chance to protect himself. He crumpled, stars exploding before his eyes. Dimly, he was aware of being seized and lifted half off the bed.

"It is not the woman Santiago is interested in, gringo," Red Sash hissed. "He sent us to deal with the *bastardo* who killed Pedro Valdez and José Gonzalez." Red Sash shook Fargo, then tossed him down. "Say your prayers, pig."

Fargo tried to marshal his thoughts but his head was swimming.

"Time to die, gringo."

3

Skye Fargo's vision cleared and he saw the bejeweled knife poised above his neck for a fatal thrust. In the twinkling of time before Red Sash struck, he realized the bandits wanted to dispose of him quietly. Gunfire would bring the hotel staff and other guests on the run.

Red Sash speared the knife downward. Fargo jerked his head to the right and the blade missed by a fraction, thudding into the carpet. As the bandit drew the weapon back for another thrust, Fargo swept both legs against the man's shins and brought Red Sash crashing to the floor.

The other *bandido* started to close in to help his friend when Virginia Ragsdale let out with a piercing scream that must have been heard from one end of Socorro to the other. The man stopped and glared. *"Silencio, puta!"*

Fargo caught all this out of the corner of an eye. He was too busy preserving his own hide to go to Virginia's aid. Red Sash had recovered swiftly and lunged, trying to rip his stomach wide open, but Fargo blocked the blow and drove his right fist into the killer's mouth. Something crunched loudly and blood sprayed in a wide arc.

Red Sash was furious. Pushing to his knees, he swung again and again.

The bandit's rage worked in Fargo's favor. The man was so mad it didn't occur to him to use his pistol. If he had, the fight would have been over then and there. But the oversight bought Fargo precious time to scoot backward, ducking and weaving as he evaded that glittering blade. Suddenly his right hand brushed an object on the floor, an object that was as much a part of him as his hands and feet. He had used it so many times that he could handle it blindfolded if need be.

It was the Colt. In a smooth, fluid blur, Fargo whipped the six-shooter up and out and squeezed the trigger twice. The slugs cored Red Sash from front to back, blowing out the rear of his skull and splattering gore on the bed and the wall.

The other bandit, though, had Fargo dead to rights. He had whirled as Fargo's hand closed on the pistol and he was on the verge of firing when the door unexpectedly crashed inward and into the room leaped Cole Barton. The Texan had both Colts out. In booming cadence they thundered, four shots in a row.

At each blast the *bandido* jerked and staggered. He fired twice as his knees buckled but his shots went wild, into the ceiling.

Gunsmoke hung heavy in the air. Fargo slowly stood.

Virginia had sat up, her back to the headboard, vastly relieved at being spared.

Barton didn't give the dead men a second glance. As would any seasoned gunfighter, his first order of business was to reload. "Sorry it took me so long, ma'am," he told the redhead. "I had to hang back some or they never would have made their play."

Fargo swung around. "You knew they were Maxwell's men all along, didn't you? Yet you never said a word to us."

The Texan never batted an eye. "Sheathe your claws, mister. I had a hunch they were part of the gang, was all. Ragsdale mentioned that one of the bandits was partial to a red sash." He nodded at the dead man in question. "I had to let them show their hand before I could act."

Fargo saw the gunman's point, but he still had the feeling the nursemaid was holding something back. "Did Ragsdale expect Maxwell to send someone to murder his daughter? Is that the real reason he hired you?"

Virginia came off the bed in a rush. "Must we discuss this terrible business right this minute? I'd like to have these scoundrels dragged out of here, and then I need some time to

32

myself." She shuddered. "In light of what has happened, I say we stay over one more night and head out in the morning."

"Whatever you want, miss," Barton said.

The prospect of a delay annoyed Fargo, but being stone-walled annoyed him more. Reluctantly, he stooped to haul Red Sash out.

In the corridor, feet drummed. The desk clerk was the first framed in the doorway. "My word!" he exclaimed. "What's the meaning of this outrage?"

"Maxwell's men," Fargo replied. "Give us a hand."

More men arrived. The bodies were lugged down the street to the undertaker's, who propped them in open coffins in front of his establishment and charged two bits apiece for viewing rights. A curious crowd gathered in no time.

Barton disappeared in the throng. Fargo headed for the hotel but changed his mind at the last minute and entered O'Keefe's saloon. Word had already spread like prairie fire. The bartender greeted him with another free drink.

Fargo accepted, but he drank a sip at a time, in no way anxious for a repeat of the night before. Some of the customers came over to congratulate him, and while they were standing around joking and pounding him on the back, Fargo remarked, "Did I hear right? Did this Santiago Maxwell grow up around here?"

"That he did," a grizzling old-timer said. "I knew his pa and ma, both. Alfredo Santiago was a farmer. Had a small place north of town, along the river. Never amounted to much, but he tried real hard."

"And the mother?" Fargo probed.

"Ruby Allen was her maiden name. She came from back East to do missionary work among the redskins. We tried telling her there was no way in hell that she could convert the Navahos, but she wouldn't listen."

Things weren't adding up. Fargo recalled Ragsdale saying that Maxwell's mother was trash, hardly a fitting description of a missionary.

"Way I hear it," the old-timer went on, "they named the

33

sprout after her father. He came to visit her once. Quiet, mousy sort of gent he was. A regular dude."

A skinny young man in a suit broke in. "Max and me went to school together. We used to play hooky down by the Rio Grande all the time. No one could hunt or track like he could."

Fargo was becoming more perplexed by the second. There was nothing in Santiago's past to account for his going bad. It sounded as if the man had been blessed with a decent pair of parents who had tried their best to rear him right. "What made Maxwell take to killing and plundering?"

O'Keefe answered. "No one really knows, mister. His folks died years ago, and for the longest time he made his living breaking horses. Did all right, too. Then, about twelve months ago, he shot a Bar R hand at a cantina on the south side of town. He skedaddled into the mountains, and the next we knew, he had turned into a crazed killer."

"And him a churchgoer!" a customer said in disgust.

The bartender motioned at Fargo. "Have you made up your mind yet about going after him? No one would hold it against you if you turned Ragsdale down. A lot of men have tried to fill Max full of lead and they've all wound up six feet under."

"I haven't decided yet," Fargo said, but the truth was that he didn't think he had much choice. Santiago had tried to have him killed and might try again at any time. Given Santiago's vengeful streak, it was entirely possible the bandit would send men clear to Las Cruces if he had to.

Further talk was cut short by bedlam outdoors. Hoofs pounded madly, wagon wheels creaked and rattled, and a flurry of shouts broke out.

Everyone made for the door. Fargo was the second one to emerge. Up the street a stage had stopped. The team was lathered with sweat and close to exhaustion. The driver sat slumped back against the luggage rack, a bright red stain high on his shirt, while the shotgun messenger had collapsed over the footboard, his body riddled with bullet holes.

Dozens of people surrounded the stage and more were flocking to the scene. Fargo hurried over and shouldered through the throng to where several men were carefully lowering the driver. The hubbub of voices hushed when one of them hollered to be heard above the racket, "Who was it, Bob? Who hit the stage?"

The driver was in agony but he gamely replied, "Who in tarnation do you think? Maxwell Santiago and his renegades were on us like a swarm of riled bees before we knew they were there. Jess got blasted to kingdom come before he could get off a shot."

"Where are your passengers?" asked the man who hollered.

Struggling to stay conscious, Bob limply waved a hand at the coach. "See for yourself."

Bullet holes dotted the body panels and doors. In many spots the wood had splintered. Large chunks had been blown away.

Fargo was a step ahead of everyone else in reaching the door. He pulled on the handle but it refused to budge. Straightening, he peered in the window and almost wished he hadn't.

There had been four passengers. Two men were drummers, judging by the sample cases beside their bodies. A young woman and a small boy had also been on board, and they lay in a corner where the woman had tried to shield the boy with her own body. All four had been shot to pieces.

"How awful!" someone said.

Words didn't do the slaughter justice. Fargo didn't linger, as many did. He had seen enough. Maxwell Santiago had to be stopped. The job in Las Cruces would have to wait.

The Trailsman went to the deserted livery and along the aisle until he came to the stall containing the Ovaro. The stallion bobbed its head and nuzzled him. Locating a pitchfork, he put hay in the stall, then found a feed bag and filled it with oats from a bin under the loft.

It seemed as if half the population of Socorro was still gathered around the stagecoach when Fargo made his way to the hotel. No one answered the door when he knocked on 208, so he went to his own room and spent the next hour cleaning his guns and honing the toothpick.

Late in the afternoon Fargo collected his belongings and headed down the stairs. He was almost to the bottom when

Virginia Ragsdale and her nursemaid appeared. She took one look at the bedroll and frowned.

"You're not leaving us, are you, Skye?"

"For the night," Fargo explained. "If Santiago is out to nail my hide to the wall, I'm not going to make it easy for him. I'll meet you on the west side of town at first light."

"If that's what you think is best," the redhead said, not sounding very pleased.

"I won't risk innocent people being caught in a cross fire," Fargo elaborated. With a curt nod he walked on past.

The Ovaro had eaten its fill and was eager for exercise. Fargo threw on his saddle blanket and saddle, tied the saddlebags and bedroll securely in place, and swung up. Rather than use the main street, he took a series of alleys and side streets eastward. He figured that Maxwell had posted men in town to keep an eye on things, but he saw no one who acted suspiciously, no one who had an undue interest in what he was doing or where he was going.

Once across the Rio Grande, ranks of mesquite closed around him. Fargo rode at a brisk pace for over a mile. Then he doubled back and watched his back trail from concealment. He didn't expect anyone to be dogging his steps, so he was all the more surprised on hearing an approaching horse.

Palming his Colt, Fargo bent low so his silhouette wouldn't be obvious. He spied a rider moving slowly along, screened by the brush. There could be no doubt the man was smack on his trail.

Moments later the man shadowing him came into the open. On seeing the rider's black clothes and studded vest, Fargo frowned. He let the Texan go on by, then spurred the Ovaro from hiding. "That's far enough."

Cole Barton spun but didn't draw when he saw who it was. Resting an arm on his saddle horn, he remarked, "Tricky, hombre. Real tricky. Maybe Ragsdale is right about you. Maybe you are the one who can stop Maxwell."

"I don't like being followed," Fargo said gruffly.

"Makes two of us." Barton pointed at the Colt. "There's no

need for the iron. I'm just doing as I was told. Miss Ragsdale wanted to know exactly where you went."

"You left her alone?"

"In the lobby, with four men to keep her company until I get back," Barton said.

"Tell her I don't like being spied on." Fargo twirled the Colt into his holster and moved alongside the Texan's dun. "You're lucky I'm not the nervous kind. You'd be dead about now."

Barton stayed at Fargo's six-shooter. "Rather handy with that, are you?"

"I'm still alive."

"Reckon you're better than me?"

It was an arrogant challenge, not a simple question. Fargo held his tongue. Experience had taught him never to give an inch to gunmen on the prod.

"I like to think that I'm the best around," Barton said in his lazy drawl. "Which I've proven time and again. Maybe I should put you to the test when this is over."

"Your choice."

Grinning, Cole Barton turned his mount and rode off toward town. "I'll relay your message to Miss Ragsdale. You stay healthy, hear? I wouldn't want anything to happen to you before I show you which one of us is the better man."

Fargo watched until the Texan was long gone. As if he didn't have enough to deal with, now he would have to be careful not to let down his guard whenever the gunslinger was around. His instincts had been right on the mark. Barton was a tried and true killer, the kind who would gun down kin if the price was right.

Only after Fargo was certain the Texan wasn't trying to circle around on him did he resume his trek into the chaparral. Just in case the bandits had more than one dog, he chose a small clearing almost entirely ringed by thorny vegetation and closed the gap by piling dead bush as high as his waist.

Fargo settled for a cold camp. He had plenty of jerky and a few hard biscuits which he nibbled on until stars sparkled overhead. Lying on his back, a blanket hiked to his chin, the Colt clenched underneath it in his right hand, Fargo mulled over all that happened since he had reached Socorro. At length sleep claimed him.

The twitter of a warbler was Fargo's invitation to greet the new day. He sat up and stretched to relieve the kinks in his spine, then rose and made up his bedroll. It was less than an hour until daylight, but he had more than enough time to get where he had to be.

At the Rio Grande Fargo stopped so the Ovaro could drink. He slaked his own thirst, moistened his bandanna, and wiped the grime off his face. As he went to climb back on, a flock of sparrows suddenly took wing thirty yards off. He looked, and owed them his life.

A man was crouched in the mesquite. Giving the stallion a hard slap on the side, Fargo clung on as it plowed into the river, making for the opposite bank. A rifle banged twice but the assassin rushed his aim and the shots were high.

Fargo's feet were dragging in the water so he used his left hand to give the pinto another smack. The bushwhacker had risen but it was too dark to see his face clearly. Not that Fargo needed to. The ambusher wore a sombrero.

Apparently another one of Maxwell's followers had seen Fargo ride out of Socorro but had lost the trail on the other side of the Rio Grande. The man must have waited all night in the hope Fargo would come back the same way. It had been a mistake to do so, Fargo realized.

Two more shots rang out as the Ovaro broke clear of the water and galloped into the underbrush. Fargo swung up, cut the reins sharply, and paralleled the river for over fifty yards.

Yanking the Sharps out, Fargo vaulted to the ground and dashed back to the Rio Grande. Crouched at the base of a low tree, he scoured the mesquite but saw no evidence of his attacker. Had the bandit fled? Or was the man stalking him at that very moment?

Tense moments dragged by. Even though he would be late meeting Virginia Ragsdale, Fargo stayed where he was. This made the third time Santiago Maxwell's men had tried to blow out his lamp, and he was damned tired of being used for target practice. That, and their other atrocities, rated special attention; he was going to hunt them down to the last man and exterminate the whole band.

Fifteen minutes later Fargo conceded that the *bandido* had left, perhaps to report his failure to Maxwell. Easing down the hammer on the Sharps, he returned to the stallion and soon spotted buildings ahead. Instead of going straight through the heart of town, he circled to the south.

The redhead and the gunman were waiting beside a rutted track which led toward the mountains to the west. Virginia was perched on a boulder. She stood, smoothed her dress, and came to meet him.

"It's about time. You said first light and I took you at your word." She pointed at the golden crown on the horizon. "You're half an hour late. I trust you have a good excuse."

Fargo related his encounter with the bandit.

Virginia was genuinely shocked. "Mercy! It sounds to me as if they won't give up until they pay you back for shooting Valdez and those others. Max probably wants to show everyone else that no one kills one of his gang and lives to tell about it."

"Max?" Fargo said. "I was right. You do know him."

"We met a few times before he turned outlaw." Virginia hastily turned, stepped to her bay, and was given a boost up by the Texan. Riding crop in hand, she brought her chestnut mare next to the Ovaro and said, "Let's go. We have a long ride ahead of us."

"How long?" Fargo thought to ask.

"A day and a half if we don't run into trouble."

Without delay they got under way, Barton once again bringing up the rear. Fargo didn't like having the quick-draw artist at his back but he didn't object. The gunny wasn't about to try anything until after Maxwell had been dealt with.

The country ahead of them was broken by wide valleys and plains, rugged mesas, deep canyons, and steep cliffs. Fargo had passed through it before and knew it fairly well. The Continental Divide wound through the middle of the region. Streams on the west side of the Divide ran into the Pacific Ocean, those on the east side into the Gulf of Mexico.

Virginia Ragsdale proved to be a superb rider. She wasn't one of those prissy ladies who had to ride sidesaddle. She forked leather like a man and rode as well as any cowhand. When Fargo complimented her, she grinned. "It comes of being a tomboy when I was younger. I was the son my pa never had. He let me have a pony when I was only seven and took me on all the roundups."

"Does your sister Jenny ride as well?"

The corners of Virginia's mouth curled downward. "She wasn't the tomboy type. Being a lady was more important to her than learning to ride or shoot or dress game. When she was a girl, she was more interested in playing with dolls and china and such."

Fargo could have cut her contempt with his knife. "I take it the two of you don't see eye to eye."

"No, we sure as hell don't," Virginia said bitterly. "We never have and I doubt we ever will. I'll be happy when Pa sends her back to Virginia in the fall to stay with his brother. He thinks the change of scenery will do her some good."

"Is she sick?"

"You might say that."

At midday they stopped beside a narrow stream to water the horses and rest. Virginia spread out a blanket in the shade of a cottonwood and took a loaf of bread and cheese from her saddlebags. "Anyone care for a bite?"

Barton shook his head.

Fargo sat down next to her and accepted a slice of each. He had a lot of questions he wanted to ask but he knew that he couldn't come right out and press her for answers or she'd clam up on him. To learn more, he had to take a roundabout approach, like a bronc buster trying to corral a contrary mustang. "How many head of cattle does your father own?"

"I think the last tally put the count at over two thousand. Not bad for a man who started out with less than two hundred."

"How many horses?"

"Several hundred or so."

"Does he break his own or buy them from someone?"

Virginia cocked her head. "Both. Sometimes he hires mustangers to catch wild horses in the high canyons and bring them down. At other times he buys from ranchers who have extra head to sell. It all depends. Why?"

Fargo leaned back and tried to sound as innocent as could be. "Someone in town told me that Maxwell used to make a living breaking horses. I was just wondering if he ever broke some for your father."

"As a matter of fact, he did. That's how I met him. He was good at it, better than anyone else in the whole territory."

"Did he beat the horses a lot?"

"Heavens no. Max wasn't cruel like some mustangers I could name. He had a knack for getting a horse to tame down without having to club it half to death." Virginia bit into her bread. "Why, once I saw him break a magnificent white stallion that wouldn't let anyone come near it. He was as gentle as a mother with a newborn babe, and within an hour he had that stallion eating out of the palm of his hand."

The more Fargo learned about Santiago Maxwell, the less he understood. Any man who treated animals kindly usually treated people the same way. What could have happened to change Maxwell so drastically? Why had the man turned into a bloodthirsty butcher?

"Might be trouble coming!" Cole Barton abruptly called out.

The gunman was gazing to the northwest. Fargo did the same and saw four riders.

All of them wore sombreros.

4

Cole Barton moved closer to the rancher's daughter, planted his feet in a wide stance, and hooked his thumbs in his gunbelt on either side of his big silver buckle. A sinister smile creased his thin lips. He had the air of a sidewinder about to strike.

Fargo knew a man like Barton was liable to fly off the handle at the least little provocation. But the four Mexicans showed no sign of being hostile. Not a one carried a rifle and all their pistols were holstered. A portly man in the lead was smiling broadly.

"Don't start anything unless they give us cause," Fargo told the gunman.

The Texan sneered. "I don't work for you, mister. I work for Ragsdale."

Before Fargo could ask what difference that made, Virginia took several steps and raised a hand in greeting. "*Buenos días*, Senor *Rivera*."

In a spray of dust the quartet reined up and the portly man tipped his sombrero. "Good morning, Miss Ragsdale. It has been too long since last we saw one another. How is your father?"

"Pa is doing fine. He'd be doing better if it weren't for Maxwell. Last week Santiago ambushed another one of our punchers and shot fifty head of cattle for no other reason than to watch them die." Virginia paused. "Has he hit your spread yet, Senor *Rivera*?"

"No, he has not, Miss Ragsdale."

"Now isn't that peculiar." The redhead glanced at Fargo. "Rivera owns a ranch north of the Bar R. He's been there for years, even before my pa settled here. He has over a dozen vaqueros working for him and close to eight hundred head, but he hasn't lost a one to Maxwell."

Barton grunted. "Sounds strange to me too, ma'am. It's almost enough to make a body suspect the two are in cahoots."

Rivera shook his head. "That's not true, senor. I am an honest man. I do not deal with butchers."

"Did you call me a liar?" Barton demanded. He took a stride and lowered his arms to his sides. "The last jackass who did that is pushing up alfalfa back in Texas."

"I meant no insult," Rivera quickly said. "My men and I want no quarrel. We are on our way to pick up a few supplies."

"How do we know that?" Barton snapped. "How do we know that you're not going into Socorro to meet secretly with Santiago Maxwell? Maybe he hides out at your place from time to time and that's why no one has been able to find him."

Rivera pulled his hat brim low and clasped his reins. "You talk foolishness, senor. I will not sit here and be insulted."

The Texan moved in front of Rivera's mount. "You'll leave when I say you can, Mex. And if you don't like it, you're welcome to fill your hand. You and all your chili peppers."

Fargo had to do something. In another moment one of Rivera's vaqueros would go for his revolver and all hell would break loose. Since the hotheaded gunfighter was to blame, he slipped up behind Barton and jammed the forefinger of his right hand into the small of the Texan's back. Barton froze. "That will be enough out of you," Fargo said.

Rivera's surprise was apparent. "My thanks, senor. Your friend must learn to control his temper."

"He's not my friend," Fargo said. "You'd best ride on before he does something we'll both regret."

Touching the brim of his sombrero, Rivera jabbed his spurs into the flanks of his horse and galloped eastward toward the town. One of the vaqueros, the youngest, hesitated, as if tempted to test Barton's mettle, but at a sharp cry from his employer, he, too, rode away.

Only when the riders were out of pistol range did Fargo back up three strides. "Turn around," he commanded.

A perfect picture of suppressed fury, Barton did. On seeing Fargo's extended finger, he snarled like an enraged wildcat and said, "Didn't anyone ever teach you not to meddle? I reckon it's time you were taught some manners, mister. So fill your hand whenever you're ready."

"No!" Virginia stepped between them. "There'll be no gunplay, Cole. Pa wants Fargo alive and that's how we'll deliver him. Understood?"

"But you saw what he did!" Barton objected. "No man makes a jackass out of me and lives. No man!"

"You made a jackass out of yourself," Fargo corrected him, and deliberately turned his back on the gunman to walk to the blanket. It was a gamble, but a calculated one. He was fairly confident that Barton wasn't about to defy William Ragsdale.

The gunman glared awhile, then stormed off, thunder hovering on his brow.

Fargo took his time finishing the bread and cheese. Virginia sat near him and kept studying him when she thought he wasn't looking. At last she made bold to speak what was on her mind.

"Why did you side with old man Rivera against Cole?"

"Your nursemaid was in the wrong."

"Who appointed you the Almighty? Cole had every right to treat them the way he did, them being what they are and all."

Fargo was fast losing his appetite. "You have no proof that Rivera is involved with Maxwell. And the last I heard, in this country a man is innocent until proven guilty."

The redhead gave out with a mocking laugh. "I never would have figured you to be a stickler for the law. Since you are, you'd better keep in mind that out here folks have been living by a different law for longer than any living person can recollect."

"What might that be?"

"An eye for an eye and a tooth for a tooth. It's the only law my pa recognizes."

The meal was finished in silence. Virginia folded the blanket and tied it to her animal. Fargo offered to help her onto the saddle but she jumped on by herself and took the lead, Barton by her side.

Fargo could take a hint. He trailed them until twilight, his bandanna pulled up over his mouth and nose to keep from swallowing their dust. Several times the pair talked in low tones and made no effort to include him. He didn't care. Once he finished with Santiago Maxwell, it would be good riddance for the temperamental Ragsdale family and their hired hardcase.

Camp was made in the foothills in a glade beside a pristine spring. From the amount of horse tracks and human prints, Fargo deduced the spot was a favorite stopping point for travelers using the trail between Socorro and the Plains of San Augustin.

Fargo made the fire without being asked. He didn't trust the other two to do it right. Most whites liked to build roaring blazes which could be seen for miles around. It was wiser to do as the Indians did and make a small fire so as not to invite unwanted guests.

Virginia brought the rest of the bread and cheese over, but Fargo was in the mood for tastier fare. Taking the Sharps, he went into the forest and spent fifteen minutes poking into brush and weeds. Presently a black-tailed jackrabbit bounded from hiding and he nailed it before it had gone fifteen feet.

Rabbit stew was one of Fargo's favorites. He skinned the animal in no time and boiled it in his own pot. He also made the coffee. Virginia and Barton watched closely, practically drooling. Both were surprised when he offered them some.

The Texan hesitated, pride fighting with hunger. "Why?" he asked bluntly. "After how I treated you today, I should think you'd rather see me starve."

"Let me put it this way," Fargo said, giving some to Virginia. "If a band of Mescalero Apaches were to jump us, would you help fight them off?"

"What a loco question. I'd have to wouldn't I?"

"Then it's in my best interests to keep you alive." Fargo sat back and spooned the stew into his mouth. The rabbit meat was done just right; plump and tasty.

Virginia tried some of hers and blinked. "Why, this is delicious."

"Shouldn't it be?" Fargo responded.

"Most men I've met couldn't cook if their lives depended on it. The average male can't boil water without burning the pot."

Fargo tilted his tin coffee cup to his mouth, then commented, "When a person has to live off the land, they learn to make do or to do without. Some frontiersmen I know can cook better meals than the finest chef east of Mississippi."

"Women's work," Barton grumbled while downing his portion with relish. "You'd never catch me doing it."

"You must go hungry a lot," Fargo said, and helped himself to seconds. They were on speaking terms again, which was an improvement, but he still didn't trust the gunman as far as he could heave a bull moose. And he had growing doubts about Virginia as well. Rivera was her neighbor, yet she had been all too willing to allow Cole Barton to gun the man down. Why?

After supper Fargo brushed down the Ovaro. He seldom did when on the trail but he was still feeling guilty over his lapse in Socorro. He had done the shoulders and was working on the flanks when soft footsteps drew near.

"Mind if I join you?"

Fargo pulled a burr from the stallion's tail, then turned. "I thought you weren't fond of my company anymore."

Her lips pursed, Virginia sat on a convenient log and crossed her long legs. "I'll admit I was a little put out with you, but I'm not one to hold a grudge. Besides, now that I've had time to think about it, you were in the right and Cole was in the wrong. I hope you'll accept my sincere apology."

The change of heart seemed legitimate, but Fargo couldn't help but note that she didn't look at him when she said it. He continued brushing the pinto.

"You care for that animal a lot, don't you?" Virginia inquired, adding as an afterthought, "Strange."

"Why should it be? You were raised on a ranch. Weren't you ever fond of a particular horse?"

"No, I meant that it's strange that a man who is so good at killing can care for anything. Barton doesn't give two hoots about his. It could keel over tomorrow and he'd just go out and buy another."

Removing another burr, Fargo remarked, "Comparing Barton to me is like comparing guns to knives. They're both used to kill people but they're as different as night from day."

Virginia leaned toward him, grinning. "Which are you? The gun or the knife?"

Over by the fire the Texan was helping himself to more coffee. Fargo finished brushing and stuffed it into one of his saddlebags. The twilight had deepened and soon darkness would descend. He spotted a few stars. As was his habit, he scanned the countryside for other fires but saw none.

"You never take anything for granted, do you?" Virginia noted.

"Not if I can help it. I'll live longer that way."

Standing, Virginia folded her hands behind her trim back and said, "I'd like to take a short walk. Would you be so kind as to accompany me?"

"Shouldn't you take your trained wolf?"

"He's not half as good-looking as you are." She boldly took his arm and led him into the trees, her dress swishing with every step, her hair flowing in the breeze.

Fargo didn't know what to make of her. One minute she wouldn't speak to him, the next she acted like a lovesick schoolgirl. He let her guide him sixty yards into the woods, then halted. "This is as far as we go. I don't want to stray far from camp."

"Your wish is my command," Virginia said impishly. Suddenly spinning, she stood so her breasts brushed his chest and arched an eyebrow. "Now where were we when we were so rudely interrupted in Socorro?"

She was as big a hussy as any fallen dove Fargo had ever known. In light of how she had acted, he was no longer as aroused by her presence as he once had been. That could change, though, Fargo reflected, with the right persuasion. He brought his hand up and covered her right breast. She smiled that seductive smile of hers but otherwise didn't move.

Fargo slowly squeezed her breast until her lower lip trembled. He tweaked the hard nipple through the fabric and she fidgeted but kept on smiling as if nothing out of the ordinary were taking place. Putting his other hand on her left breast, he gently massaged and tweaked them both. He thought she would stand there until she could no longer control herself and melt into his arms, but she had something else entirely in mind.

Abruptly, Virginia reached out as if to touch his stomach but at the last second she pressed her hand against Fargo's organ. Taken unawares, he jumped, which caused her to giggle. She began stroking him, her eyes hooded, licking her lips as a bulge formed in his pants.

Fargo sensed that she was testing him in some way, trying to see which of them would break first. Since he had no intention of being bested by her, he ran a hand down across her flat stomach to the junction of her thighs. Her legs shook slightly as he rubbed her there.

Virginia closed her eyes and rocked on her heels, her tongue visible between her lips. She moaned softly when his hand slid between her legs and his fingers molded themselves to her womanhood.

Pumping his hand briskly, Fargo felt the friction warm them both. It grew hotter and hotter until, when he suddenly jabbed his thumb into her core, she quivered and swayed, about to lose her balance. Fargo didn't let up and moments later her legs gave out. He caught her in time and lowered her to the grass. The dress hiked to her thighs, revealing exquisite legs as sheer as silk.

"Like what you see?"

Fargo would have answered her had he not been consumed by sheer lust. Sinking to his knees, he caressed her shins, her knees, her inner thighs. She rubbed his arms, then raised a hand to his head and entangled her fingers in his hair.

Flipping the hem of her dress onto her waist, Fargo exposed her underthings. Parting them, he inched a hand past her nether mound to the inferno between her legs. She was as ready as any woman had ever been but he was not going to satisfy her until he was good and ready himself. To that end, he found her tiny passion knob and tweaked it as he had her breasts. At his first touch she arched her spine and came up off the ground as if trying to leap into the air. She gripped his wrist but didn't pull his hand away.

Fargo was about to bend down when a twig snapped faintly in the trees. Suspecting that the gunman had shadowed them, he surveyed the forest. No one was there. Or so it appeared. By bending to the left he could see the fire. Cole Barton was hunched over near it. An animal must have broken the twig, he mused, and bent.

The scent of a woman at the height of passion is more fragrant than flowers, more intoxicating than alcohol. Fargo nuzzled her core and she clamped her thighs tight on either side of his head, so tight it almost hurt. He applied his tongue to where it would do the most good, eliciting a sharp squeal. She bucked and rolled her hips. He held her down and licked until his tongue was sore.

"Yesssss," Virginia breathed. "I love it!"

Kneeling, Fargo went to remove his gunbelt but thought better of the idea. Since Maxwell's men might jump him at any time, he needed to keep the Colt handy. He only loosened the belt enough to lower his pants.

The redhead wrapped her hand around his pole and sighed. "Goodness. You have enough there to split me in half," she joked.

"I aim to try."

Fargo opened the top of her dress and her swollen breasts burst free. Lowering his mouth to her right nipple, he sucked and nibbled for a while before switching to her other one. The whole time she wriggled under him and played with his member. He was so hard, it hurt.

"How much longer?" Virginia pleaded.

"Wait and see."

Planting a lingering kiss on her mouth, Fargo dropped his hands to her hips and positioned himself. When she least expected it, he thrust into her to the hilt. Virginia cried out and threw her head back, tossing it from side to side. Pausing for a few moments, Fargo held her firmly and commenced stroking. A tingle shot up his spine and his mouth went dry.

"Never stop! Never stop, lover!"

Fargo would have liked to oblige, but he was closer to the brink than he wanted to be. He paced himself as best he could, emptying his mind so he would last longer. She didn't help matters any by digging her nails into his side and raking his back from shoulder blades to hips. Biting down on his lower lip, he willed himself to keep pumping.

Moments later Virginia gripped his shoulders, gasped, and commenced slamming her hips into him as if she were trying to batter him in half.

Fargo knew what it meant. He picked up the tempo of his strokes, no longer having to hold back. Her soft belly slapped against his iron stomach while her slick thighs glued to his. Together they rocked in carnal abandon, neither aware of anything other than the supreme pleasure they were bringing to one another.

"Oh! Oh! Oh!"

The redhead's cry was Fargo's signal to explode. He drove into her with a vengeance and she clung to him mouthing feverish moans and groans which tapered in volume as they gradually coasted to a stop, fatigued and fulfilled.

The breeze cooled Fargo's sweaty form. He could feel her heart hammering, feel her warm breath on his cheek. In the distance an owl hooted. Elsewhere a coyote yipped and was answered by others of its kind.

For a little while Fargo could permit himself the luxury of relaxing. Danger wasn't present. There was just the two of them.

And whatever made another twig snap in the forest.

Sitting up, Fargo groped at his side for the Colt. Unable to find it, he feared it had fallen during their lovemaking, but it was only hidden by a fold in his pants. Drawing the pistol, he listened.

Virginia seemed to be sleeping. Fargo rose, adjusted his clothes, tightened the gunbelt, and cat-footed closer to the nearest trees. He had a better view of the fire and the gunman.

Barton hadn't moved. He also spotted someone or something forty yards away, slinking toward the camp.

Dashing to Virginia, Fargo shook her shoulder. She mumbled but failed to awaken so he shook her harder. When she opened her eyes, he said, "Get dressed quickly."

"Why are you in such a rush?" Virginia asked. Sitting up, she yawned. "I would have liked to rest awhile longer."

"We're not alone out here," Fargo warned.

Anxiety came over her and she swiftly complied. Once she was on her feet, Fargo grabbed her hand and hastened back. The clumsy stalker was between them and the fire and he recognized the outline of the man. Halting behind a trunk, he debated his next move. By rights he should yell to alert the Texan. But if bandidos were ringing the glade, they would cut loose the instant he did.

"Do you think they saw us?" Virginia whispered.

Fargo had no idea, but given the noise they had made, he couldn't see how the bandits had missed them. And if that was the case, why hadn't the killers slain them? Hastily removing his spurs, he slid a hand into his boot, pulled out the Arkansas toothpick, and held it out. "Take this."

"What for?"

"To protect yourself. Stay right here until I let you know it's safe to come out."

Virginia clutched at him. "Wait! Where the devil do you think you're going?"

"I can move faster and quieter by myself," was all Fargo said, and he was off, gliding along with all the speed and skill of an Apache, bounding like a nimble buck over obstacles.

The stalker had stopped and appeared to be watching the gunfighter.

As Fargo ran, he was alert for the others bandits. He was convinced there had to be more than one, so he was all the more puzzled when he spotted none. Twenty yards from the figure, he slowed. Crouching, he advanced cautiously. He narrowed the gap to ten yards and could tell the figure wore a sombrero. It clinched his suspicion.

Avoiding the ground under trees, where twigs were likely to

be found, Fargo closed on his quarry. He could have shot the man dead but held his fire. Meanwhile he searched right and left, yet still could not discover any more *bandidos*.

Then the figure moved, and the pale glow of dancing firelight glinted dully off a metal object in the man's hand. It was a revolver. He was taking aim at Cole Barton.

The Texan picked that exact moment to rise and stretch his legs. He walked in a small circle around the fire, glanced absently into the trees, scratched his chin, and sat back down in a different spot.

The man in the sombrero had held his fire but now moved close to a pine and took precise aim.

Fargo had five yards to cover. He intended to take the bandit alive in order to learn where Santiago Maxwell was hiding out. Hefting the Colt, he sprang, his arm upraised to club the figure. But he was not quite close enough to swing when the man must have heard him and whirled.

The night was rent by the boom of a pistol.

5

Skye Fargo stared death it its cold metal single eye. He saw
the man spin, saw the six-shooter swing up and out, and knew
he was a dead man because there was no way he could swat
the barrel aside before the man fired. Then the gun banged.
Fortunately for him the man in the sombrero rushed his shot
and the slug missed by a fraction.

Before the bandit could snap off a second shot, Fargo was
on him. Fargo brought the butt of his Colt crashing down on
the killer's sombrero and the man flopped to the earth like a
puppet whose strings had been snipped.

Cole Barton had dived flat at the retort, his Colts flashing
out of their holsters. He was looking for a target but he was
handicapped by being so close to the fire that everything beyond the radius of its glare was an inky veil.

Fargo ducked low and called out to prevent the Texan from
blazing away at random. "Don't shoot, Barton! It's me,
Fargo!"

"What the hell is going on?"

That was a good question. Fargo scoured the woods but saw
no other *bandidos*. Apparently the one he had slugged was the
only one. "Hold on," he said. "I'm coming in." Sliding his
hands under the unconscious bandit's shoulders, he dragged
the man into the circle of firelight.

The killer's sombrero had slipped over his face. One arm
twitched, as if he were trying to lift it even in his state. His pistol dangled from his trigger finger.

Fargo scooped the six-gun up and wedged it under his belt.
"He was fixing to shoot you."

Barton had stood. He glanced at the bandit and frowned.

53

"You saved my life?" An odd look came over him. "Damn, mister, I wish you hadn't done that."

Fargo knew that expecting the gunfighter to be grateful was too much to ask. But the complete lack of appreciation rankled him. "Next time I won't."

At that juncture the underbrush crackled and someone raced out of the darkness.

Both Fargo and Barton snapped their hardware up and were ready to drop the newcomer in his tracks when they saw that it was Virginia Ragsdale. She had torn the bottom of her dress and was out of breath but none the worse for wear.

"I told you to stay put," Fargo mentioned.

The redhead shrugged. "If you hadn't learned by now, I do as I please, when I please. And I wasn't about to stay out there alone." She poked a foot at the killer. "Is this another one of Maxwell's gang?"

"Let's find out," Fargo said as he stooped and lifted the sombrero. He didn't think he would know the man but he was wrong. It was the young hothead who had been with Rivera.

"It's Diego," Virginia said. "Hernando Rivera's youngest son."

"Well, I'll be," Cole Barton said. "That pup had more grit than I gave him credit for. I reckon I ought to send him back to his old man draped over his saddle with a note saying how sorry I am that I had to put windows in his skull." Smirking, he pointed one of his Colts and slowly cocked the hammer.

The Texan's attitude was understandable. Bushwhacking was the vilest of acts. It ranked with horse stealing as the most despised crime on the frontier. But Fargo couldn't just stand there and let the young man be shot. "We should take him back to Socorro and turn him over to the law."

The gunfighter hefted his Colts. "Out here, *these* are the law. Don't tell me that you wouldn't want to kill him if he had tried to gun you down."

"I'll admit that I would," Fargo said, stepping in front of Diego Rivera. "But this isn't the way to handle it."

Virginia moved closer to the Texan. "Don't listen to him,

Cole. I say you're within your rights, and my pa will back you up. Do what you have to."

Barton glanced at her, then down at the young man. "Damn!" he growled, and shoved his pistols into their holsters.

"What are you doing?" Virginia demanded, snatching the gunman's sleeve. "Don't let him talk you out of it. Shoot!"

"I can't," Barton said.

"Why not?"

"Fargo stopped the kid from killing me."

"So?"

Barton jerked his arm free. "Do I have to spell it out for you? Fargo saved my bacon."

The redhead was confused. "Does this mean that you have to do everything he says? Does he call the shots from now on, or do you still work for my pa?"

"I'll still do as your pa wants," the Texan said.

"Then shoot Diego—" Virginia began, but stopped when the younger Rivera groaned and opened his eyes. Sneering at him, she cracked, "Welcome back to the world of the living. You don't know how close you came to becoming worm food."

Rivera looked at each of them, his expression a blank stare. His befuddled senses were slow to sharpen. He attempted to sit up but his hand slipped out from under him. *"Que pasa?"* he mumbled.

"Don't play innocent," Virginia said. Bending, she gripped his hair and shook him. "When my pa hears what you've done, he'll be fit to be tied. He's warned your pa a dozen times not to buck us Ragsdales. Seems to me you would have learned your lesson by now."

Fargo seized her arm and pried her hand loose. "That's enough," he said. "Can't you see the knock on his noggin has him woozy."

Virginia wrenched away from him. "That's right. Take up for the Mex again. Makes me wonder whose side you're really on."

"I figured we were all on the same side, against Santiago Maxwell." Fargo knelt and helped Diego to sit. Rivera thanked him, then picked up the sombrero and gingerly felt his head.

On touching a bump on his temple, his eyes lit with recognition and he gasped, then looked around for his pistol.

"I have it," Fargo said, moving back a step. "And you won't be getting it back anytime soon. You have a lot to answer for."

"What would you have had me do, gringo?" Diego declared. "You saw how the *pistolero* treated my *padre*. Should I overlook his insult, as my father wants me to do? I say no! Never! The *pistolero* must die."

"From ambush?" Fargo said. "That's the lowest of the low in any man's book."

Diego started to stand but sank back down when Cole Barton swung toward him. "I would be a fool to challenge this *pistolero* to a *duelo*. He would kill me before I could clear leather."

The gunfighter laughed, a sound like a cold blast of arctic air on a winter's day. "You've got that right, pup. You, your pa, the whole Rivera clan wouldn't stand a prayer against me. And then where would your mother and sisters be?"

Fargo was watching Diego closely to keep the firebrand from doing anything rash, but he was taken unawares by the violent explosion brought on by Baron's comment. Rivera surged to his feet and attacked, his arms outstretched, his fingers hooked to claw into Barton's throat.

"Leave them out of this, *bastardo*!"

As quick as Diego was, the Texan was quicker. Barton drew and smashed Diego across the face, pistol whipping the hothead in the blink of an eye. Diego dropped like a rock, straight into the fire. Neither Barton nor Virginia Ragsdale made any attempt to haul him out, so Fargo leaped in close to the flames and yanked Rivera clear before Diego's clothes could ignite. Blood trickled from the young man's right cheek. Once again he was out like a busted lantern.

"You should have let him burn," the redhead said.

Fargo stared at her, and it was as if he saw her for the first time. He'd pegged her as having a hard edge but figured it stemmed from her vanity. Seeing her now, with her finely chiseled features highlighted by the pale glow, he beheld a mask of hatred so intense it rendered her lovely face ugly. He

56

realized her arrogance sprang from deep within her, from a soul so twisted and spiteful it was doubtful she would ever change.

"Why are you looking at me like that?" she demanded.

"No reason," Fargo fibbed, and dragged Rivera to where his saddle and bedroll were piled. "I'd like my knife back," he said to Virginia, and once she forked it over he took a short length of rope from his saddlebags, cut it in half, and bound Diego hand and foot.

Barton sat and poured a cup of coffee, which he gave to Virginia. She had an air of baffled anger about her. Taking a long sip, she said, "So let me be sure I understand this, Fargo. You aim to tote that trash clear to the Bar R?"

"I do."

"Why bother. Let Cole have him and spare yourself the aggravation."

"It won't be any bother," Fargo said. After getting coffee for himself, he sank onto his haunches. "I take it there are hard feelings between your father and Hernando Rivera."

"Smart man," Virginia said sarcastically.

"What brought it about?"

"Rivera never did cotton to my pa settling where he did. Rivera was here first, and he thought he had the God-given right to claim all the land for himself. My pa showed him otherwise, and ever since there's been bad blood between the Riveras and us."

Fargo remembered how friendly Hernando had been that morning and suspected there was more to the strife than she was letting on. "Has any blood been spilled?"

"Not yet, but it's only a matter of time. My pa has taken as much as he intends to. He thinks Rivera has been helping Max, and I agree." She paused. "Santiago has to have a base where he lays low on occasion. Pa suspects that it's on the Rivera ranch."

"There's plenty of wilderness for a gang to hide out in."

"Oh, Max does that, too. But there has to be someone supplying him with ammunition and supplies and whatever else he needs, and that someone is Rivera."

"Does your father have proof?"

Virginia snorted. "You never cease to amaze me. Who needs ironclad evidence? Pa has a hunch it's Rivera and his hunches are never wrong. He's going to see to it that Rivera pays."

Fargo could see where she got her headstrong nature, and that arguing with her would be a waste of time. So he drank and held his peace. Little else was said for the longest while. Eventually, Barton and Virginia turned in. Fargo stayed awake, wondering what in the world he had gotten himself into. Having to contend with Maxwell was enough of a headache without being caught in the middle of a range war between the Bar R and Hernando Rivera.

The flames dwindled as the hours dragged by. Close to midnight Fargo turned in. He slept through until shortly before dawn. None of the others so much as stirred when he rose to quench his thirst. He led the horses to water and saddled the stallion.

The aroma of half a pot of freshly brewed coffee brought Cole Barton around. He gave a curt nod on rising and drank sullenly. "I don't suppose you've changed your mind since last night?" he asked after a while.

Fargo shook his head.

"Too bad. I'm going to be raked over the coals by Ragsdale for this. I wouldn't be surprised if he up and fires me." The gunman briefly gnawed his bottom lip. "You'd be doing us both a favor if you'd mount up and ride out. I'll say that I never saw you go. No one will ever know what happened to you."

"I aim to see this through to the end."

Barton sighed. "Figured as much." He checked to insure Virginia still slumbered, then said in a low voice, "Listen, Fargo. You saved my life so I owe you. And I'm telling you here and now that you'd be smart to skedaddle while you can. There's more at stake here than you know about."

"So I guessed. What, exactly?"

The Texan opened his mouth but immediately closed it when the redhead rolled over and sluggishly propped herself

58

on an elbow. "It's morning already? Why is it I feel as if I didn't sleep a wink?" Throwing her blanket off, she patted her rumpled hair and said, "No wonder women hate mornings. We look like scarecrows when we first wake up." She smiled sweetly. "What were you boys just talking about?"

"Nothing much," Barton answered much too hastily. "Why don't you get prettied up so we can be on our way. With a little luck we can be at the ranch by noon."

Virginia was her usual pleasant self. "Don't ever tell me what to do, Cole. You were hired by my pa to look after me, which means you're to do as I say, not the other way around."

The gunman didn't try to hide his resentment. "I'll abide a lot of abuse from you, lady, but don't cross the line. So what if your pa hired me? I can quit at any time."

Fargo had to chuckle. "Another day is off to a friendly start." He splashed water on Diego Rivera to revive him. The young man's face had swelled up like an overripe melon and one of his eyes was black and blue. "Care for some coffee?"

"*Si*," Rivera said thickly. "*Gracias*"

Shifting so he could untie the firebrand's hands, Fargo froze on hearing a squirrel chatter madly off in the forest. Animals made sounds for different reasons, and squirrels were more vocal than most. They chattered when playing, chattered when courting, and chattered when angry. When they spied a predator or humans roaming their domain, they also chattered, exactly as the squirrel Fargo had heard. He pivoted to scan the trees. As he did, a rifle cracked and the bullet bit in the dirt inches from the embers.

Cole Barton and Virginia jumped to their feet.

"No one will move!" a voice called out in a heavy Spanish accent. "Not if you all want to live!"

Ignoring the order, the Texan drew his Colts and cut to the left, toward a thicket. He had taken but two steps when a pair of rifles blasted, chipping the earth in front of him. Stopping dead, he hunted futilely for the men who had fired.

"Put down your pistols, gunfighter!" the voice directed. "I do not like to shoot a man when he has no chance to defend himself but I will make an exception in your case if you do not listen."

Fargo had made no move to bring his revolver into play. For one thing, he knew the men in the trees had the advantage. For another, he recognized the speaker. So did Virginia Ragsdale.

"Senor Rivera, is that you?"

"It is, senorita. I am coming in. Tell the *pistolero* and the other one not to try anything or something will happen that we will all regret."

In a few moments the heavyset rancher appeared. His hands were empty and he made no move to draw his revolver. At the edge of the glade he halted, gazing sadly at his son. "Thank the Lord you are still alive, Diego. Do you have any idea how worried I was?"

Virginia had been rattled by the gunfire, but now that she knew who was to blame she had regained her usual sauciness. "You're loving son tried to bushwhack Mr. Barton here. Yet I seem to recall that a while ago you claimed the Rivera family weren't backshooters."

The elder Rivera stepped over to the younger. "From ambush, my son? You disgrace me. Not only do you disobey me, but you stoop to the same level as Ragsdale's hired killer."

Barton bristled. "Now hold on, mister. I've never shot anyone in the back in my life. When I drop them, they're always looking me right in the eye."

Rivera sank to one knee to untie his son. "Do you tell yourself that makes a difference, gringo? When we both know that you are lightning with your guns, and that those who look you in the eye have no chance at all?" He tugged at a stubborn knot. "No, you are like the Apaches. You kill because you like to kill, like a wolf that has gone loco."

"I'm not like no stinking Injun!" Barton said.

Fargo saw that Hernando Rivera could not quite manage the knot, and stooped to help. The rancher was surprised but did not object. The rope fell off and Fargo undid the loops around Diego's ankles.

"This makes twice you have helped me, senor," Hernando said. "I am in your debt."

"Who isn't?" Barton threw in.

Father and son rose and moved toward the trees. "Do not seek to follow us," Hernando advised. "My vaqueros long to end your lives, and it is all I can do to keep them from riddling you with bullets."

Virginia took a step and gestured. "This isn't over, Hernando. Once my pa hears, he'll be coming for you."

Rivera's sadness deepened. "I hope not, senorita, for all our sakes. The mountains and valleys will run red with blood, and when it is done, we will all be losers."

"The Ragsdales never lose."

Fargo was glad to see the father and son get away. The older Rivera struck him as a decent man doing his best to avoid setting off a powder keg. William Ragsdale, on the other hand, struck him as being downright bloodthirsty. The more he learned about the man, the less he looked forward to stopping at the Bar R.

As soon as the Riveras were out of sight, Barton picked up his Colts. "That old fool didn't know when he was well off. Now his goose is cooked, for sure."

"Meaning?" Fargo asked, but received no answer. They broke camp and were soon under way, sticking to the trail as it wound down out of the forested slopes to the plains of San Augustin. From there they followed it southward toward the base of the San Mateo Mountains.

Here and there were herds of cattle, some large, others not. At one point half a dozen hands busy rounding up cows stopped work long enough to ride over. When the punchers discovered it was their employer's daughter, they fell all over themselves to be polite. Virginia treated them as a queen might treat her subjects.

The layout of the ranch was similar to many Fargo had seen. A large ranchhouse was nestled between a pair of foothills. To one side stood a stable with an attached corral. Adjacent to it was the long, low bunkhouse.

The ranch bustled with activity. A bronc buster was breaking a mustang in the corral, cheered on by companions. A man in a blue cap was trimming hedges which had been planted in neat rows bordering the porch. On top of the stable a man was repairing a weather vane.

Fargo took all this in as he neared the sprawling house. He was so intent on seeing who came out to greet them that he almost missed spotting the young woman who came out of a chicken coop over on the far side of the stable. She was as lovely as Virginia but as different as day from night. Golden hair cascaded over slender shoulders. A yellow dress molded to a full figure that would turn heads in any town. She had blue eyes which must have sparkled when she was happy, but at that moment she walked as one doomed to be executed, as sorrowful a sight as Fargo had ever seen. Why that should be, he had no idea.

"Is that your sister?" Fargo asked.

Virginia turned and frowned. "That's her. Little Miss Goodness herself."

"Is she ill?"

The redhead snickered. "Don't I wish. No, she's been moping around the place for months now. Yet anther reason for Pa to send her back East. I'm so tired of seeing that hound dog look, I could scream."

Fargo was passing close to Jennifer Ragsdale. He touched his hat brim and gave her the friendliest smile he could muster. Her gaze was as empty as a dry well. To prompt a response, he said, "Hello, Miss Ragsdale."

Jennifer stopped and started as if she had been pricked with a pin. "Hello," she said meekly. " I don't believe I've had the pleasure of your acquaintance."

"Skye Fargo, ma'am."

Further talk was slashed short by the slamming of the front door. Out of the building had walked the king of the roost himself, William Ragsdale. He had a thick cigar clamped in the corner of his mouth, and his red shirtsleeves were rolled up to his elbows, revealing his rippling muscles. "My baby!" he cried in delight at Virginia, then opened his powerful arms wide and beckoned.

The redhead slid off her mount and dashed up the steps. She

flung herself into her father's embrace, receiving a big hug as she was spun in a circle.

"So how did it go?" Ragsdale asked. "Any problems?" His daughter whispered a few words. He let her go and looked up. "Cole, you might as well get some rest. We won't be needing you the rest of the day."

The Texan made for the bunkhouse.

Ragsdale looked at Fargo and was about to say something when he noticed his other daughter, who had stopped near the porch rail. "What the blazes are you doing there, girl? Get inside with those eggs. Your ma needs them for supper tonight and it's not polite to keep her waiting."

"Yes, Pa," Jennifer said timidly, scooting up past him and to the door, where she paused to glance once at Fargo. Then she was gone.

Fargo dismounted and arched his back to relieve a kink. He promised himself that before he left the Bar R, he would find a way to talk to Jennifer alone. Boots clumped on the steps and he turned toward Ragsdale as the man came down off the porch and halted in front of him. A puff of cigar smoke was blown into his face.

"I heard tell that you can lick your weight in bobcats," Ragsdale declared. "And I'd like to see you prove it."

6

Skye Fargo tensed and clenched his right fist. He took the remark as a challenge and braced himself in case the rancher tore into him. But instead, Ragsdale clapped him on the arm.

"If you can track down Santiago Maxwell and put an end to his rampage, I'll be in your debt for the rest of my born days. I guess you heard about the stage? One of my men was in town and rode out to tell me." Ragsdale shook his head. "Tragic. Just tragic. I ask you. What kind of man brutally kills a mother and her little boy?"

For some reason, Fargo was reminded of the many patent medicine men he had heard trying to convince skeptical listeners that their products were all they claimed. Ragsdale was trying to sell him on the fact that Maxwell had to be eliminated. "I've already made up my mind," he clarified, "I'm going after the gang in the morning."

The rancher beamed. "You have no idea how glad I am to hear you say that. Anything you need, you just ask. Ammo, guns, vittles, whatever, I'll see that you get it. And my men are completely at your disposal. Take as many along with you as you want. They're all dependable and good shots. Anyone would do to ride the river with."

"I work alone."

Ragsdale clucked. "Better reconsider. No one knows for sure how many guns Maxwell has riding with him. Some say ten. Some say fifteen or more. Pretty stiff odds for a man to buck on his lonesome."

"I'll keep your offer in mind," Fargo said, but he wasn't about to change his mind. The punchers would be more of a hindrance than a help. Few cowhands were skilled trackers, and fewer still, despite their rowdy ways, were a match for hardened gunmen. Then, too, traveling with a large bunch of riders would slow him down, plus make it next to impossible to sneak up on Maxwell's gang.

An older hand had walked over from the stables and was standing close by. Ragsdale turned to him. "Charley, I want you to take care of Mr. Fargo's horse. See that it gets all the feed and water it needs, and give it a rubdown."

Fargo removed his saddlebags and yanked the Sharps out of the boot before giving over the reins. "I'll sleep in the stable tonight," he said. "I don't want to put your family out in any way."

"Nonsense." Ragsdale steered him toward the porch. "The missus and me love to have company. There are plenty of spare bedrooms for guests. And it will be nice to have a new face at supper. Maybe you'd favor us with talk of your travels. Bess and I don't get to do much ourselves, much as we'd like to. Running the Bar R is a twenty-four-hour-a-day, twelve-months-a-year proposition."

A wide hallway led into the interior of the house. The first room was a lavishly furnished parlor, the next a den where the rancher did his books.

"I do my own ledger work," Ragsdale declared. "Bess is always after me to hire an accountant, but only a fool trusts a stranger to keep track of his own money."

Hanging on the wall were the stuffed heads of a mountain lion, a bear, and a buck. Ragsdale walked over to the black bear and patted it. "Look at the size of these critters. And I killed them all myself. One shot each, right through the heart."

The rancher stepped to a large bobcat which had been mounted in a crouch, with one paw raised to strike. "This ornery cuss grew fond of chicken meat. Made off with eight of my wife's prized hens before I was able to tree it and bring it down. Gave me a hell of a chase. So out of respect, I had it stuffed whole."

At a junction, Ragsdale bore to the left and they shortly entered the kitchen, where Jennifer stood cracking eggs into a bowl. An older woman was taking flour down from a shelf. She had a soft, kindly face and many gray streaks in her hair.

"Skye Fargo, I'd like you to meet the apple of my eye, Bess. We've been married going on thirty-five years."

The woman wiped her hands on her apron and offered one to Fargo. "It's a pleasure to meet you. Bill tells me you might put a stop to all the horrible killing."

"I'm going to try." Fargo saw Jennifer looking sideways at him and smiled. She grinned meekly in return, then bent to the bowl when her father glared at her.

"There's no time for dawdling, girl. I want a proper feed tonight in honor of our guest. Whip up some of those honey cakes I like so much."

Bess Ragsdale sighed and patted her daughter's arm. "You've no call to be so bossy, Bill. Jenny is working hard. She's been helping me out all day."

Ragsdale snorted. "About time she pulled her own weight. We can't have her wasting her life away reading those fool books she's forever burying her nose in, or writing poetry hour after hour. Life is work, not all play, and it's about time she realized as much."

The young woman's shoulders slumped, and Fargo felt a twinge of resentment over how she was treated. His feeling grew when the other daughter waltzed into the kitchen a second later.

"Ginny!" Ragsdale exclaimed happily. "There's no need for you to help out. You probably want to freshen up before we eat."

"I'm fine, Pa," the redhead said, bestowing a smug look on her sister. "And there's a lot we need to talk about. Right now, if we could."

"Whatever you want." The rancher nodded at his wife. "Bess, why don't you show Fargo to his room while Ginny and I go to my den. Give a holler if you need anything."

Father and daughter departed arm in arm.

The mother nudged Jennifer and said, "Why don't you show Mr. Fargo to his room, sweetheart, rather than me? I'll mix the batter while you're gone."

"But Pa told you to do it. I don't want to rile him."

"Don't fret. I'll tell him it was my idea. Just run along."

The blonde sheepishly gestured at Fargo and headed out. He felt sorry for her but didn't feel it was his proper place to meddle in their affairs. "Nice spread your family has here," he commented. "How do you like ranch life?"

"I love it," was her barely audible reply.

"Your sister told me that you'll be heading to Virginia to stay with your uncle in several months. Are you looking forward to it?"

Jennifer abruptly stopped and twisted, her face betraying fear. "Did she tell you why Pa is sending me back there?"

"No."

The woman went on, leaving Fargo to ponder why she had acted so scared. The way she acted, the way she moved, reminded him of a frightened doe ready to bolt at the first glimmer of danger. Yet here she was in her own house, among her family, the safest place she could possibly be. It made no sense to him.

"Maybe we'll have the chance to go for a ride sometime," Fargo proposed. "You can show me the Bar R."

"I'd like to, but I couldn't. Pa would never let me."

Fargo couldn't stop himself. "Aren't you a little big for your father to be telling you what you can and can't do? A grown woman should be able to live her life as she chooses."

Again Jennifer stopped and looked at him, her gaze drilling into him as if she were trying to see into the depths of his soul. "A person would think so, wouldn't they?" was her cryptic response.

The bedroom was spacious and airy. A large window opened on to a grassy tract. There was a large closet flanked by a polished chest of drawers. Fargo placed his saddlebags and rifle on the bed and commented, "Your folks have done themselves proud. Half the hotels I've stayed in weren't near as nice as this."

"They do work hard," Jennifer said. She had stayed by the door, nervously running her hand along the jamb. Caught in the light streaming in through the window, she was like a golden angel, her smooth features practically shining, her flaxen hair as radiant as the sun.

Fargo found it remarkable that she had not married yet. Virginia, too, for that matter. Women were at a premium on the frontier. Beautiful women, more so. Both sisters should have suitors lined up in droves. To test his hunch, he said, "You must have a gentleman friend somewhere who will be awful sorry to see you leave."

Jennifer bit her lower lip, then said quietly, "I did have an admirer once. It seems like a lifetime ago."

"Just one? You?" Fargo laughed. "Things will change in Virginia. Southern men flock to pretty women like bears to honey. You'll have to beat them off with a club."

The blonde smiled. "Oh, pshaw!" Then, unaccountably, she quickly backed up and said, "I'd better return to the kitchen. I don't want Pa catching me here. It was nice meeting you." In a swirl of her dress, she was gone.

Fargo had no desire to stay cooped up in his room. He decided to go check on the Ovaro. As he passed the den door, which was closed, he overheard Ragsdale and Virginia talking. The rancher sounded mad.

"—should have known better. What if he had guessed? Not everyone feels the same way we do. Some are just too dumb to see the light."

"I did what I thought was best."

"Forget it. I'm more concerned about Barton. I was told he's as reliable as the day is long. This has to be looked into. I'll go have a talk with him when we're done."

That was the last Fargo heard. Mulling over what it might mean, he crossed from the house to the stable. The bronc buster was busy with a different horse and fewer cowboys lined the corral. Inside the stable the odor of hay and horse droppings was strong. His saddle had been draped over a stall. He saw the man called Charley repairing tack in a small room on the right and walked over. "Thanks for tending to my horse."

Charley started and nearly dropped the bridle. "Damn, mister, you gave me a scare! I didn't hear you coming. You must move like an Injun." He cocked his head. "Not that it will help you much against Max if you go after him."

"Who told you I might?"

"Hell, everyone on the Bar R knows by now. I wouldn't be surprised if Max himself has heard that you're coming after him. He has ears everywhere."

Fargo sat on a barrel. "You've been around awhile, I take it. What can you tell me about Santiago?"

"The man has snake blood in his veins. If you were to drop him into a rattler hole, the snakes wouldn't put up a fuss because they'd think he was one of their own."

"I hear he wasn't always mean. He used to break horses, didn't he? Someone told me he even worked for Ragsdale for a while."

"That he did. Busted horses here for, oh, about nine or ten months. And he was good at it, too. One of the best bronc squeezers I'd ever seen and I've been around a spell." Charley grinned wistfully. "You should have been here. Max had the knack in spades. He could tell which way a horse would jump before the animal knew itself. And when he was thrown, he knew just how to kick free of the stirrups and go limp when he fell so that he never broke a bone. 'Course, there weren't many cayuses that could throw him. He hung on as if glued on."

"If he was so good, why did he give it up and take to killing and robbing?"

Old Charley went to answer but clammed up when a shadow fell across them.

William Ragsdale was framed in the doorway, a new cigar clamped in his mouth. "Thought I heard your voice," he said to Fargo. "What are you doing out here?"

Fargo stood. " I wanted to stretch my legs."

"Well, I'll thank you not to distract the help from their work," the rancher said pleasantly. His eyes narrowed toward the stableman. "As for you, Charley, you have too much work to do to waste time jawing. I expect to have that bridle fixed before the day is done."

"It will be," Charley said testily.

Ragsdale stepped to one side so Fargo could go past. "I swear, that man would talk the ears off a jackrabbit. He's a handy man to have around but at times he does try my patience." He pointed at the entrance. "Come along. There's someone I'd like for you to meet."

A cowboy waited just outside. He was lean but muscular, his work clothes caked with dust, his neck sweaty. He showed about as much friendliness as a Comanche on the warpath when the rancher led Fargo over.

"This here is my foreman, Bo Weaver. He's been with me four years now, and I couldn't ask for a better right-hand man. I've told him that anything you want, you're to get. Say hello to the man, Bo."

Weaver merely grunted.

Why the cowboy should be so hostile, Fargo had no idea. But he wasn't surprised. It was just another peculiar circumstance in the long chain of baffling events which had started when the three *bandidos* and the dog had tried to bushwhack him.

"If you don't mind, I'd like for Bo to show you around," Ragsdale said. "It won't take long. By the time you're done, supper should be about ready." Nodding to the foreman, he headed for the house.

Bo Weaver acted as if he'd just been told to jump buck naked into a cactus patch. "Follow me," he grumbled, making for the corral.

Fargo didn't budge. "If you'd rather not do it, that's fine by me."

The foreman halted, then stared at Ragsdale's retreating figure. "It's not that," he said gruffly.

In no mood to mince words, Fargo said, "Then why are you treating me like I just killed your best friend?"

Weaver came closer. "All right. You want the truth, I'll give it to you, straight tongue." He jabbed a finger at Fargo's chest. "I don't want you getting any ideas about Ginny Ragsdale. We've been sweet on one another for pretty near six months. I aim to wed her before the year is out. And no saddle tramp is going to come between us."

The insult hung in the air like a threat. Weaver became bolder when Fargo offered no answer.

"I talked to that Texan. He says Ginny and you were right friendly on the ride out from Socorro. I want to know *how* friendly."

"It's none of your business," Fargo said, and began to go around.

"Like hell it isn't! You'll tell me, saddle tramp, or some of the boys and me will persuade you to make yourself scarce from these parts, pronto. What's it going to be?"

Fargo hit him. Without saying a word or giving any sign of what he intended to do, Fargo belted the man on the jaw. Weaver staggered back into the wall, feebly tried to bring his fists up, then collapsed, his eyes rolling upward.

A snicker drew Fargo's head around. Charley had stepped from the tack room and was grinning. "What's struck your funny bone?"

"Weaver. He's the biggest pain in the ass who ever put on britches. It's nice to see someone put the uppity bastard in his place."

"Was he telling the truth about Virginia Ragsdale?"

"Who can say? Just between you and me, that filly is trouble. She likes to break men almost as much as Max liked to break horses. I've lost count of the number of men who have come calling and gone away with their hearts in their hands." Charley nodded at the foreman. "This fool is just the latest in a long line who thought they had won her hand. Every last one was left with an empty palm."

Fargo left the foreman lying there and walked out to the corral. The bronc buster had snubbed a mustang to a post and was putting on the bridle. The horse balked, throwing its head back and nickering. Fargo leaned on the rail to watch but then spotted Jennifer Ragsdale hurrying from the house toward the chicken coop, a basket crooked in one elbow. He managed to get there just as she came out. "Hello again."

Jennifer hesitated. "Mr. Fargo. Whatever are you doing here?"

"Call me Skye. I came to carry the basket for you." Fargo

took it from her and waited for her to proceed. She glanced at the house, swallowed, and nodded.

"I don't need the help, but I thank you for your kindness. Most everyone else around here tends to ignore me." She nervously smoothed her dress, then put her hands behind her back. "Ma needed more eggs. Supper will be ready in about an hour. I hope you like chicken and dumplings."

"I do." Fargo walked slowly, in no hurry to part company. He had an urge to get to know the shy, awkward beauty better. She was the one person who might be able to shed some light on what Ragsdale was up to.

Jennifer went to speak but closed her mouth. Once more she tried but she couldn't seem to muster the nerve. Finally she took a breath and blurted, "Why do you want to kill Santiago Maxwell?"

Of all the questions she could have asked, that one took Fargo by surprise. "It's not as if I came to Socorro looking to kill him. But something has to be done. You must know about the many people he's butchered. He has to be stopped."

"Maybe he'll stop on his own."

"A man like that? I doubt it. Even if he does, the law won't rest until he's behind bars or hanging from a gallows." Fargo saw her jaw muscles twitch.

"You're not a marshal or sheriff. Wouldn't it be best to let them handle it?"

Fargo sensed that she was in great turmoil but he couldn't imagine why. "They've tried," he pointed out. "But most lawmen are town bred. They're no match for a man who can live off the land like an Indian and vanish into the wilderness whenever they close in."

The blonde frowned and said, "They should just leave him alone. Everyone should." She suddenly took the basket and hastened on ahead of him.

The door slammed shut behind her. Wondering what in the world he had gotten himself into, Fargo walked around to the porch and sat on a bench. He felt as if everyone he met was hiding something from him, and he was growing tired of being played for a fool.

Presently Ragsdale came to tell him supper was about to be served. Everyone else was already seated at a long mahogany table in the dining room. In addition to Mrs. Ragsdale and the sisters, Cole Barton and Bo Weaver were on hand. The latter sported a large bump on his chin, and when asked about it by Ragsdale, Weaver claimed he had been kicked by a horse.

Everyone made small talk except Fargo. The dumplings were perfect and he was starved. No one pestered him with questions so he was the first one done even though he had seconds of everything. Pushing back his plate, he reached for his coffee.

The rancher was lighting another cigar. He blew a few smoke rings into the air, then looked down the table at Skye. "Ginny told me what happened at the Excelsior. You must carry a rabbit's foot around with you, the charmed life you lead." He took another puff. "She also told me about Hernando and Diego Rivera. You shouldn't have interfered."

"I did what I had to do."

"From your point of view, I suppose you did. But as my daughter told you, Rivera and I aren't on the best of terms. He's despised me from the day we first met."

"Why?"

Ragsdale glanced at his wife, who averted her face. "For the life of me, I don't know. I've done my best to be a decent neighbor, but that's not enough for some. I suspect he's just envious. He wanted this land for his own."

Such rivalries were common. Many Mexican landowners had been outraged when Mexico gave up its right to the territory, and resented the influx of Americans who poured in afterward. Fargo could see where Rivera might hold a grudge, but from what he had seen, Hernando was a peaceable man who wanted to avoid a clash.

"Now about tomorrow," Ragsdale was saying. "Is there anything you need? How many men are you going to take along? Bo can have ten ready to ride at first light."

"I don't need any supplies," Fargo said, "and I told you before that I work alone."

"At least take Clay. You'll need someone to keep an eye on

your back trail. The last man who went after Maxwell alone was found with a bullet hole between the shoulder blades."

"No."

A strained silence gripped the group and did not let up until after dessert, when Fargo excused himself. Although he was sure Charley would take good care of the Ovaro, he went to the stable and idled away twenty minutes doing nothing but rubbing the stallion's neck and scratching behind its ears. The cowhands were all in the bunkhouse eating their own supper so he had the place to himself.

That is, until Fargo turned to go. Furtive footsteps warned him he was no longer alone. He strode to the middle of the aisle as Bo Weaver and two husky punchers blotted out the twilight. He didn't have to ask why they were there.

The foreman smirked as he advanced. "You didn't think that you had seen the last of me, did you? That lucky punch you landed earlier doesn't hardly count."

"You're a jackass," Fargo said.

"Am I? I saw the way Ginny looked at you during supper. I want to make damn sure that when you ride out tomorrow, you never come back."

The three men raised their fists.

7

Skye Fargo could have drawn and shot all three men before any of them reached him. But in doing so he would have taken unfair advantage since not one of them made a move to unlimber a revolver. They planned to teach him a lesson, to beat him into submission. So he waded into them on their own terms, his first blow clipping the overeager foreman and sending Bo Weaver tottering back into a stall.

The husky pair had been picked for their boxing savvy. They closed in from opposite sides. The puncher on the right, who wore a thick mustache, feinted, then delivered a straight right which Fargo ducked. Even as he did, Fargo grabbed the puncher's wrist, pivoted, and hurled him into the second cowboy, who was just cocking a fist to strike. Their legs became entangled and down they went, cursing mightily.

Fargo knew he had to keep on the go, that he dared not slow up for an instant or they would have him. He pounced on Weaver as the jealous fool was straightening. A jarring jab to the ear knocked Weaver off balance and he fell.

Before Fargo could press his advantage, the other two regained their feet and charged. This time they were side by side, seeking to overpower Fargo by their momentum and weight. But he was not so easily taken.

Diving at the ground in front of them, Fargo bowled both cowboys over. The one with the mustache caught himself and only fell to his hands and knees. Shifting, he lashed a backhand which would have knocked Fargo near senseless had Fargo not caught the movement out of the corner of his eye and blocked it with a forearm.

Putting both hands flat, Fargo swung his entire body into a

swift arc, driving his boots into the man's face. He felt the nose give, heard a distinct crunch. The man howled like a stricken timber wolf and scooted backward, a hand pressed to his spurting nostrils.

Meanwhile, the foreman had risen, and now sprang. Weaver tackled Fargo, his arms locking around Fargo's chest, and they crashed down with Weaver on top. Smiling in triumph, Weaver whipped his right arm on high to punch Fargo in the face. Quickly Fargo resorted to a head butt, ramming his forehead into the other man's mouth.

Weaver cried out and rolled to the left, allowing Fargo to push upright. He was just in time. The other cowboy tore into him with fists flailing and it was all Fargo could do to block the flurry of punches.

Backpedaling, Fargo gave as good as he got. He was hit on the chin and the shoulder. Neither did much damage. In retaliation, he landed a solid right to the puncher's cheek and a sweeping left to the man's stomach.

Sputtering thickly, the puncher staggered to one side, desperately trying to catch his breath.

His intuition screaming a warning in his brain, Fargo whirled. None too soon. Bo Weaver had picked up a pitchfork. Snarling like a berserk beast, the foreman lunged, seeking to impale Fargo on the tines. Fargo danced to the right, grabbed the handle, and tried to wrest the implement free. Weaver stubbornly hung on, and for a few seconds they swung back and forth, neither able to prevail.

Abruptly reversing direction, Fargo drove the end of the handle into the pit of the foreman's gut. Weaver grimaced but would not let go. So, doing just that, Fargo skipped in close and slammed a solid right to the foreman's head, which dropped Weaver like a rock.

Fargo drew back his right fist to finish the man, but a heavy body plowed into him from the rear. He was thrown into a pile of hay, which cushioned the impact. A knee gouged into the base of his spine and heavy fingers tore into his neck. Exerting all his strength, Fargo shoved high enough off the floor to drive his elbows back into his assailant. One of them connected with the man's ribs and the grip on Fargo's neck slackened.

Fargo had the break he needed. Wrenching to the right, he tore loose. The cowboy with the broken nose swore and swung but he hadn't set himself and the blow glanced off of Fargo's arm. Fargo made no such mistake. His knuckles blistered the puncher's head and face three times in the blink of an eye.

The cowboy reeled backward to save himself.

Fargo's reprieve was short-lived. Bo Weaver was erect, blood dribbling from his chin, a wild gleam lighting his eyes. "You son of a bitch!" Weaver screeched, and leaped, the pitchfork cleaving the air in front of him.

Behind Fargo was a stall, to his left the pile of hay. He had only one way to go, to the right. But Weaver could see that and would be anticipating the move. So Fargo pretended to go to the right but hurtled to the left at the very last moment. The pitchfork whizzed past his head.

Growling, the foreman swung, bashing the handle into Fargo's shoulder in an effort to send Fargo sprawling. But Fargo braced his legs, snaked an arm over the handle, and spun while holding on tight.

Weaver, unprepared, was whirled into the stall so hard one of the planks cracked with a sound like a gunshot. He held onto the pitchfork and shook his head to clear it.

Fargo had to dispose of the foreman before the punchers recovered. He took a step and gave a short hop. In midair, he drove his boot into the side of Weaver's neck. The foreman crumpled wordlessly.

As Fargo came down, the hired hands were on him. A hail of blows battered his head and shoulders. He hiked his arms above him to ward off most of the punches, focused on the chin of the cowboy with the mustache, and let the man have it with all the power he could muster. It was enough. Mustache flew into a stall and buckled.

Only one cowhand remained. He retreated a step, assumed a boxing stance, then struck as Fargo was rising. They clashed, trading precise blows. The puncher slipped a hook, tried to slam into Fargo with his shoulder, and received a solid right to the jaw that staggered him.

"What the hell is the meaning of this?"

The roar of outrage froze Weaver and the punchers in place. Fargo, breathing raggedly, bruised and sore, glanced up the wide aisle to where William Ragsdale and Cole Barton stood. The rancher was livid, his mouth a grim line. Ragsdale stalked forward with those ham-sized fists of his clenched so tightly his knuckles were white.

"Did you hear me? Someone had better have a damned good explanation!"

The cowboy with the mustache was closest to the door. "We were just doing as Bo wanted, boss," he croaked through cracked lips.

"Is that a fact, Isley?" Ragsdale said, and hit the man. It was a short punch, yet it lifted Isley clear off his feet and dumped him senseless.

The other cowboy immediately lowered his arms. "Yes, sir," he said anxiously. "He told us we had to help him teach this hombre some manners."

"And you did as he told you without first checking with me?" Ragsdale reached the man and made as if to swing, then gestured angrily for the puncher to step aside. The man exhaled in relief and skipped out of his employer's path.

Bo Weaver still held the pitchfork. He looked down at it, aghast, and cast it to the ground. As Ragsdale swept toward him, he blurted, "I can explain, boss! Honestly I can!"

Ragsdale glanced at Fargo. "I'd rather hear him tell his side of it. What happened?"

Fargo hesitated. If he admitted the truth, Ragsdale would probably give Weaver the pounding the foreman so richly deserved. Or maybe fire him. But Fargo didn't care to be beholden to Ragsdale for anything, and he certainly wasn't about to have Ragsdale fight his battles for him. "We were sparring for the fun of it," he said with a straight face.

William Ragsdale did a double take. "Sparring?" he said. "Do you think I was born yesterday? The four of you were trying to kill each other."

Fargo had said all he was going to. He touched his mouth, where the clean-shaven cowboy had caught him a good one, and when he drew back his hand, there were drops of blood on his finger. "I'm turning in," he said. "Tell Charley I'll be riding out at first light."

A spasm in Fargo's shoulder made him wince as he headed past the startled foreman. As he came abreast of Ragsdale, the rancher seized his arm.

"Hold on , damn it. I want the truth out of you."

Fargo stared at Ragsdale's hand until Ragsdale removed it. Not saying a word, Fargo went on, past the Texan, who was grinning broadly. Once outside, he sucked in the cool air. Stars were out, and the northwesterly breeze had picked up, as it usually did at that time of day.

The women were on the porch, gazing worriedly at the stable. Bess Ragsdale was shocked when saw Fargo approach. "Goodness gracious, Mr. Fargo! Whatever happened to you?"

"I made the mistake of standing too close to one of your donkeys," Fargo said while climbing the steps. Virginia, saw, seemed amused by the shape he was in. Jennifer, on the other hand, was as horrified as her mother.

"But . . . but we don't have any donkeys," Bess declared.

"You'd be surprised, ma'am." Fargo tapped his hat brim, then went on in. In his room, he used a washbasin, which had been provided, to clean off his face and then lay on the bed with the damp cloth on his brow.

Fargo had to get an early start in the morning, so he wanted to enjoy a good night's sleep. But try as he might, he was unable to fall asleep. The fight had set his blood to pumping like mad, and for the life of him he couldn't calm down again. Several times he got up and paced to work off excess energy. And every so often he went to the window to stare out at the heavens.

Fargo heard some of the others turn in, heard them say good night and the sound of their doors closing. Soon the big house was as quiet as a tomb, yet still sleep eluded him. He slid off the bed one more time and stepped to the window.

Off in the dark, something moved.

Instinctively, Fargo crouched so that just his eyes were above the sill. It took a few seconds for them to adjust to the deeper dark of the outdoors. When they did, he made out the shapes of a person leading a horse by its reins, heading eastward between the two foothills which flanked the house.

Fargo could tell the person was trying to sneak away undetected. It could well be a cowboy going to visit a sweetheart at a neighboring spread, he reflected, but somehow he doubted it. Then the person turned to look back at the ranch a final time and golden tresses shone faintly in the starlight.

It was Jennifer Ragsdale.

Quickly Fargo left his room. He ran into no one else on his way to the front door. The Bar R lay silent under a mantle of sparkling stars except for the yip of a distant coyote. He half expected the stable doors to be barred but they swung out easily.

The Ovaro had been sleeping. It came awake instantly when Fargo reached its stall. He had the stallion saddled in short order and led it from the building. No one had noticed. The bunkhouse was dark; no doubt all the cowboys, including Charley, were in dreamland.

Fargo imitated Jennifer's example and walked the Ovaro until he was far enough from the house to insure that none of those there would hear when he rode off. He swung up, then tilted his head, listening. From the northwest came the dull drum of hooves.

The blonde had circled wide around the buildings, a precaution Fargo likewise took. He had to stop every so often to listen for the sound of her mount, and hoped she was so intent on reaching wherever she was going that she wouldn't hear his.

For the better part of an hour Fargo trailed the younger sister northward, back along the same trail that had brought him to the ranch. When the trail bore eastward, she continued to the north. He thought she was heading for the Galinas Mountains, but she veered due east after a time, into the San Mateos.

Fargo had no doubt that Jennifer had a specific destination in mind, but where it could be puzzled him. If she had been heading to Socorro, she would have stayed on the trail. So far as he knew, the nearest ranch was the Rivera spread, which he had been led to believe was much further north.

She had to be meeting someone, Fargo mused. But who? And why so late at night? It had to be someone important for her to risk the wrath of her father. One possibility occurred to him, but he dismissed it. She hadn't impressed him as being a woman in love. Still, there was no telling.

Her course wound upward across a series of slopes which grew steeper the higher they climbed. Most were covered with trees so Fargo had no problem staying hidden. But one was a talus slope, where there was no place to take cover, and where he had to pick his way with exquisite care. It slowed him down, so much so that when he came to the top and stopped to listen, he heard nothing other than the wind.

Worried he had lost her, Fargo moved a few yards to the south, then to the north. He heard her again, the clomp of hooves on stone. Resuming the chase, he shortly came over yet another crest and discovered a mountain valley tucked away in a natural bowl rimmed by stark peaks.

Across the valley a rider was visible. It had to be her. Fargo stayed where he was until she had gone into the pines, then he followed, bent over his saddle so his silhouette would not be as obvious. The high grass helped to hide him, but not enough for his liking.

At the tree line, Fargo stopped. No hoofbeats broke the tranquillity. He was about convinced that he had lost her when a horse whinnied no less than a hundred yards off. Hopping down, he put a hand over the Ovaro's muzzle to keep it from answering. When it made no attempt, he guided the stallion into dense brush and tied the reins to a branch.

Near the spot where the horse had whinnied stood a squat square patch of black which Fargo suspected was a building, a line shack used by punchers sent to tend summer herds grazing the high country. He crept toward it, the reassuring feel of the Colt in his right hand, the Arkansas toothpick rubbing his ankle.

Fargo's hunch panned out. Forty feet from the front door he spied two horses ground-hitched at the side of the cabin. One had to be the blonde's. But who was the owner of the other mount?

All too aware that he might be making a jackass of himself, Fargo snuck forward. If he was wrong, if she did have a lover, he would get out of there just as fast as he could. Then he heard a voice, a *man's* voice, and he paused behind a tree trunk. The words were muffled by the walls but the speaker's slight Spanish accent was not.

On the same side of the cabin as the horses was a small window. It had no glass, no curtain. Fargo moved toward it. He closely watched the two animals, ready to hide if they nickered in alarm, but one was a stallion and the other a mare and they were too interested in one another to give him a second glance. He crouched under the window to eavesdrop. Now Jennifer was talking.

"—wasn't important I wouldn't have done it. I don't understand why you are so upset with me."

No one said a word for a bit. Then the man sighed. "The truth? The reason you brought me here is not that urgent. I think you gave the signal just to see me. This new bounty hunter will suffer the same fate as all the rest."

"But that's just it," Jennifer argued, "he isn't a bounty hunter. And he's different. More dangerous. I can see it in his eyes." She paused. "When Pa came home three days ago and told us he had met a man who might be good enough to stop the raids, I felt the same as you do now. Inside, I laughed at him, thinking of all the times I had heard those same words before. But then this man came to the ranch with Ginny and I met him. His name is Skye Fargo—"

"Fargo!" the man exploded. "Why didn't you say so in the first place? He is the one my men told me of, the one who killed Pedro and José and Pepe. Felipe tried to ambush him at the river, but he got away. This one is a devil, a *diablo*. This one I will take very seriously."

"Then I did the right thing, Max?"

"*Sí.* You did the right thing."

Fargo couldn't believe his ears. Jennifer had ridden all the way from the ranch in the middle of the night to meet Santiago Maxwell! She cleared her throat.

"Surely this proves to you how much I care? I meant it when I said that I would never stop loving you. Just say the word, Max, and we'll flee to Mexico right this minute. All we need is the love in our hearts and the clothes on our backs and we can make a clean start down there. You're not wanted south of the border."

There was a rustling noise, and Fargo heard a sharp intake of breath.

"Don't do that!" Santiago said. "How many times must I tell you that it is over between us before you will accept that it is?"

"You don't mean that," Jennifer said, "or else you wouldn't have shown up tonight. You came because you still care, whether you're willing to admit it or not."

Santiago came close to the window. Fargo scarcely breathed, his gaze locked on the opening.

"Hear me out, Jenny, for old time's sake. *Por favor*."

"I'm listening."

The bandit's spurs jangled as he started to pace. "I was not going to come tonight. I hoped that if I did not, you would at last accept that what we had is finished. But I could not take the coward's way out. I had to come and tell you to your face that this is the last time we will ever meet. Even if you hang the red towel on the line, I will not meet you."

"But—" Jennifer began.

"I am not done," Santiago said harshly. "Yes, we had something once. Yes, I loved you. But now my heart is as cold as the snow on the mountain tops. Your father taught me well, and it is a lesson I will never forget."

Jennifer gave a low sob. "How can you let him win? How can you let him separate us? You're playing right into his hands."

"I don't care. He will be dead before long, and then I will have paid him back for the scars." The bandit laughed bitterly. "Maybe, before I rip his heart from his chest, I will thank him for opening my eyes. I should have seen the truth sooner but I was blinded by the words of my parents, who taught me that all people can live together. What fools they were!"

"Don't give up—"

Whatever else Jennifer said was drowned out by a tremendously loud whinny uttered by the black stallion. Fargo automatically glanced at it to see if he was the cause. The mare had turned away from the stallion to offer herself, and the male horse had become excited. So he wasn't to blame. But the harm had been done.

Santiago Maxwell's head popped out of the window and an oath burst from his lips.

Fargo glimpsed a tanned face, a sweeping mustache, and dark eyes. He swiveled and pointed the Colt upward but the bandit had already leaped back inside. Swiftly Fargo threw himself to the right. As he did, a pistol cracked twice and the wood below the sill exploded outward. The shots had been angled just right. If Fargo had still been standing there, he would have been killed.

Twisting onto his back, Fargo was about to return the favor when he realized he might accidentally hit Jennifer Ragsdale. So he held his fire and scrambled to his feet while inside boots thumped and Maxwell shouted.

"You *puta*! You are no different than all the rest! You were the bait to lure me into a trap!"

"No! I swear!"

Fargo heard a ringing slap. Feet pounded, nearing the door. Springing to the corner, Fargo trained his revolver, waiting for the *bandido* to show himself. Maxwell did, but he held Jennifer in front of him and had his pistol pressed to her temple.

"Your choice, gringo. If you want her to die, shoot."

It wasn't much of a choice. Fargo had to stand there helplessly and watch Maxwell back rapidly toward the far corner, using the blonde as a shield. Maxwell reached it, laughed, and gave Jennifer a rough shove while leaping from sight. Jennifer slumped to her knees, her head bent, her features shrouded by her long hair.

Fargo was not about to let the butcher get away. He sprinted toward the same corner, intending to reach it before Maxwell reached the rear of the cabin. But as he was about to go by Jennifer Ragsdale, her head shot up and she flung herself at his legs. Her arms wrapped tight around his shins. He couldn't stop in time and down he went.

"No! No!" she wailed. "I won't let you kill him! I won't!"

Fargo tried to kick free but she clung to him in desperation. "Let go, damn it!" he fumed, and pushed her, to no avail. She clasped her arms harder.

"No! No!"

A commotion on the other side of the cabin told Fargo that Maxwell had reached the horses. Saddle leather creaked. In moments the most wanted man in New Mexico would escape. Although Fargo had no desire to be rough with Jennifer, he grabbed her right wrist and yanked. She cried out but still would not release him.

Just then hooves pounded. Santiago Maxwell galloped into the open in front of the cabin instead of into the brush, which surprised Fargo until he saw why.

Maxwell snapped the pistol up to fire.

8

At the very instant Santiago Maxwell extended his arm, the skittish stallion bobbed its head and pranced to one side. It threw off the bandit's aim, keeping him from firing.

It also bought Skye Fargo a few precious seconds. "Look out!" he yelled, and tried again to push the clinging woman from him while at the same time he pointed the Colt.

Jennifer Ragsdale looked. And she did let go. But instead of rolling aside, she clutched his gun hand.

Fargo jerked his arm back and hurtled to the right as Maxwell fired twice. One of the slugs ripped into the soil within inches of Fargo's head. He banged off two shots of his own, but between having to ward off the blonde and the stallion's antics, he knew that he had missed.

Maxwell fired one last time. Spurring his mount, he streaked into the trees and was gone.

Fargo started to rise to run to the Ovaro and give chase when he noticed Jennifer lying on her side, an arm outflung, as still as a log. Suspecting a ruse, he rasped, "Get on your feet! It won't work." He headed across the cleared space but took only four steps when he glanced over his shoulder and saw her still lying there. A dark stain marred her pale features.

Drawing up short, Fargo listened to the crash of the stallion as it sped northward. "Damn!" he fumed, and ran back to Jennifer. Crouching, he confirmed the stain was blood seeping from a shallow furrow in her temple. The last shot of Maxwell's had creased her.

Fargo angrily shoved the Colt into his holster, looped his arms under Jennifer, and carried her into the line shack. Puffs of dust rose from under his boots, proving the place hadn't seen regular use in a long time. But there was a table, a chair, and a small stove. He placed her on the former, bending her legs so she wouldn't slip off. From his ankle sheath he took the toothpick and cut a strip from the bottom of her dress.

Line shacks were seldom located far from water. Fargo dashed outside and made a circuit of the building. A few yards from the southeast corner glistened a small spring. He hurriedly soaked the strip, then ran back inside.

Jennifer hadn't moved. Fargo wiped her face and cleaned the wound. Near as he could tell, it wasn't life threatening. Going to the pool again, he cleaned the strip and cupped water in his free hand.

A low groan filled the shack as Fargo entered. He let the cold water trickle between Jennifer's parted lips and she sputtered, coughed, and then sat bolt upright. Which was a mistake. Moaning, she swayed and would have pitched to the floor had he not caught hold of her. She pressed a hand to her temple and sagged.

"Sit still,"Fargo directed. "You were hit."

Her response was a slur of words spoken so softly they were impossible to make out.

"I'll lay you back down so you can rest," Fargo said. Easing her flat, he dabbed at the wound, which continued to seep a small amount of blood. Jennifer was staring at him but her eyes were wide and unfocused, like those of a drunk. "It's a flesh wound, no more," he informed her. "You'll hurt like hell for a few days, but in a few weeks you should be as good as new. Just take it easy until then."

Marshaling her will with visible effort, Jennifer declared, "You shot me! How could you?"

"Maxwell did."

"Liar! He wouldn't harm a hair on my head!"

Jennifer's outburst provoked more anguish. She cried out and cringed, her eyelids fluttering. Fargo placed the damp strip on her forehead. "I tried to warn you. But you're as hardheaded as your father."

It had been an innocent remark, yet it so aroused Jennifer that she half rose off the table and glowered at him in sheer spite. "Don't ever compare me to him! I'm nothing like he is! Do you hear me? Nothing!" She faltered, gasped, and swooned.

Fargo was ready. Catching her lightly, he lowered her yet again and commented, "You would do both of us a big favor if you would just rest quietly for a while. There are better times to throw a fit than right after you've been shot."

His humor was wasted. Jennifer was unconscious, her chest rising and falling in an even rhythm. In respose her face was like an angel's, framed by the golden halo of her lustrous hair.

Fargo left her to fetch the Ovaro. Along the way he replaced the spent rounds in the Colt. No sounds came from the forest, reassuring him that Maxwell was long gone.

After tying the Ovaro close to the spring, Fargo lugged his saddle and bedroll indoors. He spread out his blankets in one corner, fashioned a pillow using his spare buckskins, and gently transferred Jennifer from the table to the makeshift bed. She had stopped bleeding but her temple was discolored and swelling badly. He trimmed a longer strip from her hem, soaked it, and wrapped it around her head to serve as a bandage. It was the best he could do under the circumstances.

The next half hour was spent gathering wood for the stove, which he piled beside it. He kindled a small fire and left the door open so they would have some light. Then, propping his back against the wall near the front door, with the Sharps across his legs, he allowed himself to drift asleep.

Fargo slept fitfully. The least little noise would awaken him. Twice he rose and made a circuit of the shack. Not once did Jennifer stir. He checked on her several times and learned she had developed a high fever.

It seemed as if the night would never end but at long last a band of pink heralded the new day. Fargo's first order of business was to make coffee. Figuring she would be hungry when she came around, he prepared a broth using jerky and water.

About the middle of the morning, as Fargo stood leaning in the doorway, Jennifer woke up. She touched the bandage, then her temple, then gave him a withering look.

"Now I remember. You shot me."

"Think again," Fargo said wearily. "I was in front of you, remember? You were looking right at me when you were hit, and my gun wasn't pointed anywhere near you. The slug clipped you from behind."

"I don't care what you say. I don't believe you."

"Examine the wound. Is it deeper near your ear or out near your eye?" Moving to the stove, Fargo poured some of the broth into a tin cup and took it over.

Jennifer was feeling the furrow, her lips pursed in uncertainty. "I still don't believe you," she said, but her tone lacked conviction.

"Why? Because you're in love with Maxwell?"

"I am not!"

Fargo motioned at the window. "That's not what I heard. You were practically throwing yourself at the man and he didn't want anything to do with you."

"You were listening to us?" Jennifer bleated, aghast. "Why, that's obscene! You're no gentleman!"

"I never claimed to be." Fargo wagged the cup. "Are you going to take this or should I drink it myself?"

She sniffed loudly and scrunched up her nose. "What is it?"

"Poison. I made it just for you." Chuckling, Fargo returned to the doorway to stand watch. While he doubted the bandit would come back, he wasn't taking anything for granted. It would be afternoon, if that, before the woman would be fit enough to ride. Until then he had to stay alert.

Jennifer was a study in indignation. "You're a mean, despicable person, Skye Fargo. At first I thought you were nice, but now I see that it was all an act on your part so I'd lead you to Santiago." She swallowed some of the broth, then looked at it as if she couldn't believe it wasn't the foulest, bitterest concoction ever made.

"Drink the whole cup," Fargo coaxed. "You'll feel better if you do." He spied movement off across the valley, which turned out to be a small herd of grazing deer. He was tempted to go after one but wouldn't put it past Jennifer to try and ride off while he was gone.

Sulking, the blonde complied. When she had finished the

cup she set it down and remarked, "I'll bet you can't wait to tell my father."

"Why should I? What you do with your life is your affair," Fargo said.

Jennifer appeared not to hear him. "If you do, he'll tan my hide. He's always liked to take a switch to us, ever since we were out of diapers. If it wasn't for Ma, he'd have used his whip on us by now, just like he did on poor Max."

Fargo's interest perked up. "When did this happen?"

Sorrow was mirrored in her eyes when she looked up at him. "If I confide in you, will you help me?"

"How?"

"By taking Max alive instead of killing him." Jennifer held up her hand when he went to answer. "I know what you're thinking. That it's insane for me to even ask. But once you hear my story, I'm confident you'll agree it's for the best."

The woman struck Fargo as being one of those who lived in their own little world, a dreamer who thought that everyone else should see things the same way she did. If she wasn't careful, one day reality would come crushing down on her with all the weight of a mountain, and she would never be the same again. That was the nature of life. Either a person adapted or they were chewed up and spat out like so much spoiled meat. "I'll listen, but I won't make any promises."

Jennifer reflected awhile. "I guess that's fair enough. I'll have to trust my intuition, which has never been wrong before."

What about Maxwell? Fargo almost said. Instead, he told her, "Start at the beginning."

"All right." Jennifer struggled to sit up, then propped herself against the shack. "It all began shortly after Max came to work for my pa. He was hired to break mustangs, and Ginny and I used to go out to the corral every day to watch him." Her face lit up. "Oh, he was magnificent! You should have seen him. So handsome, and so graceful and quick. I think Ginny and I both became quite fond of him, but of course she would never admit as much or treat him with anything other than contempt."

"Why not?"

"Because he's not white."

Suddenly more pieces of the puzzle fit into place. Virginia's treatment of Rivera, her wish to see Diego dead, Fargo saw them all in a new, even more disturbing light. "Go on."

"Don't blame her, Skye. She comes by her attitude honestly. Pa is the same way. Fact is, he's worse. As long as I can remember, he's hated Mexicans and Indians and half-breeds for no other reason than the color of their skin."

"That's why he wants to drive Rivera off."

"Yes. Mr. Rivera has bent over backwards to be nice, but Pa won't have none of it. He's vowed that before he goes to meet his Maker, he'll rid the plains of San Augustin of every Mexican around." Jennifer paused. "Ma isn't like him. She's always tried to live by the Good Book, to treat all folks the way she'd want them to treat her. I take after her more than I do my pa."

"About the whipping?" Fargo prompted.

A cloud came over her. "I don't rightly know what got into me. I mean, I knew how Pa would act, but I went and encouraged Max. I started slipping out to see him every chance I got. We went for long rides off in the hills and had a lot of long talks. It was so grand."

Fargo could see where the story was leading and he felt sympathy rise in him for the poor dreamer whose happiness had been shattered by her father's bigotry. "The two of you fell in love."

Jennifer nodded, smiling wistfully. "That we did. Hook, line, and sinker, as the saying goes. For months we carried on, keeping it secret from everyone. I suppose after a while I grew careless. One day Ginny followed me and caught us. Of course, she hurried back to the ranch to tell Pa." She groaned once more, but not from physical pain. "It was awful. We rode back and snuck in close to the corral. No sooner did we climb down than a bunch of the hands were all over us. Pa came around the corner of the stable with his bullwhip in his hand, and I knew right then that something terrible would happen."

There was no need for Fargo to prompt her again. The words spewed out in a heartbroken rush.

"Two of the punchers held Max while another took his gunbelt and stripped off his shirt. I pleaded with Pa to let him go, to send him packing unharmed. I promised I'd behave if only he wouldn't lay a finger on Max. But Pa ignored me. It was as if I wasn't there." Jennifer closed her eyes. "He walked up to Max and called him all manner of vile names. Then he slapped Max, again and again and again."

"Was you sister there?"

"She sure was. Standing over by the stable, grinning like the cat that just ate the canary. I called out to her. I begged her to stop Pa or to go fetch Ma, but all she did was stand there and smile. That's when I saw that she's just as bad as Pa." Jennifer paused. "She always did take after him."

Fargo had heard enough. He saw no need for her to go on, to dredge up memories best forgotten, and said as much.

"I don't mind," Jennifer said. "I've tried to shut the nightmare from my mind since the day it happened, but maybe it's best to get it out in the open, to talk about it some." She looked at him. "Pa had Max tied to the fence rails. Then he moved up close behind Max and used that whip of his, peeling the flesh right off Max's back. It was horrible beyond words. I don't know how long the whipping went on because I fainted. When I came to, Max was lying in a pool of blood. Pa had him thrown onto his horse and told him that if he ever set foot on the Bar R again or tried to get in touch with me, Pa would have him killed. Then he slapped the horse and that was the last I saw of the man I loved until months later."

Across the valley, the deer suddenly scattered, bounding in all directions as if in flight from an unseen predator. Fargo watched them closely.

"We started to hear rumors of a bandit gang raiding homesteads and killing travelers. No one knew who was leading the gang until a man named Garrity survived an attack. It was Max, he claimed. And since Garrity had hired Max a few times to break horses, there could be no doubt."

Fargo put a foot outside and rose onto his toes to see a bit farther. Several of the deer had stopped and were staring alertly to the west.

Jennifer never noticed. "I couldn't believe it at first. Max wasn't a cruel man. Yet after a while I had to face facts. He had turned renegade."

A black speck appeared in the distance. Then another, and another. Fargo counted five of them and saw the dust they were raising.

"Pa rubbed it in every chance he got. So did my sister. They seem to delight in making my life miserable."

The specks grew in size. They were riders making a beeline for the line shack. Fargo would have liked to hear the rest of her tale but he was not about to stay there and be a sitting duck. Dashing to Jennifer, he bent and hoisted her to her feet, saying, "Company is coming. We have to lay low until we see who it is."

"Maybe Max is coming back for me," she said hopefully.

"Or maybe it's your father."

"Oh God. Please don't let it be him. He'll beat me within an inch of my life."

"No, he won't," Fargo vowed, and she gave him a strange look. He had to strain to hold her up, she was so weak. The riders were closer but not yet close enough to see them. Or so Fargo hoped. With the blonde shuffling bravely beside him, he got her around the corner to the mare.

Fargo leaned the Sharps against the shack so he could boost Jennifer into the saddle. She blanched and had to grip the saddle horn or she would have fallen. "Hold on," Fargo urged. Reclaiming the rifle, he took the reins to both animals in his left hand and guided them into the timber to a gully thirty yards up the slope.

"I want you to stay here and be quiet," Fargo ordered as he lowered her to a patch of grass. "Don't let the horses stray off."

"What will you be doing?"

"I want a look at our visitors." Fargo went to leave but she grabbed his hand.

"If it's Max, please don't kill him."

"That will be up to him."

Moving rapidly now that he was on his own, Fargo retraced his steps to a cluster of brush adjacent to the front of the line shack where he hunkered to await the riders. He would have liked to retrieve his saddle but they were too close.

Five cowboys trotted into the clearing and reined up. In their lead was none other than Bo Weaver. The foreman held up an arm, warily scanned the area, then dismounted. Drawing his revolver, he walked to the open door and poked his head inside. Once he saw that it was empty, he darted in.

One of the punchers was staring at the roof. The tendrils of smoke spiraling from the stove chimney told Fargo why. It also made him want to kick himself. The smoke could be seen for miles.

Fargo had known Ragsdale would send out search parties once the rancher found his daughter and guest were missing, but Fargo hadn't counted on any of the searchers traveling so far to the north.

Weaver stepped from the cabin, the strip of dress Fargo had used to wipe the blood from Jennifer in his right hand. He waved it and stated grimly, "She was here. This is from one of her dresses." Stuffing it into his pocket, he gestured. "That saddle tramp's rig is inside, so he was with her. Spread out. Find them."

Fargo couldn't let them do that. If they stumbled on Jennifer, she would be put through sheer hell. They would drag her back to face her father, who might beat her as he had so many times before. She needed time to mend and he aimed to give her that time.

Holding the Sharps in his left hand, Fargo stalked from the brush and stopped near the corner of the shack. "That won't be necessary," he announced.

At the sound of his voice, Weaver and the rest whirled. Weaver was the only one who had his gun out. The others clawed at theirs but made no move to clear leather when they saw that Fargo was not threatening them,

"You!" the foreman barked.

Fargo made no sudden moves. He'd rather avoid trouble if he could. "Ride on back to your boss and tell him that his daughter will be home soon enough."

Weaver gazed past him. "Where the hell is she?"

"Safe."

"Bull!" the foreman snapped, and pulled the strip of material out. "There's blood on this. Something has happened to her. For all we know, Jenny's dead. Take us to her, now."

"I'd rather not," Fargo said.

"You don't have any choice, mister." Weaver brought up his pistol and thumbed back the hammer.

The man was right. Since Fargo wasn't about to lead them to the gully, he had to discourage them from hunting for her on their own. So as Weaver took a bead, Fargo drew and fired from the hip, ripping a slug through the foreman's shoulder. He bounded around the corner as the four cowhands came to Weaver's aid. Their shots peppered the side of the shack, chewing wood, spitting slivers.

Fargo was in a tight fix. He had to drive them off without killing them and without being gunned down in the bargain.

Weaver was on the ground, thrashing. A lanky puncher had leaped down and was rushing to help the foreman. The others provided cover fire. Fargo aimed at the man who had dismounted and shot his hat from his head. Then, skipping backward to avoid another volley, he sped around the rear of the building to the south side.

The cowboys were still tightly bunched and still pouring gunfire at the wrong corner. The lanky hand had dragged Weaver to his mount and was trying to lift the foreman high enough for Weaver to step into the stirrups. But Weaver was not helping out. His head lolled from side to side and he kept sputtering orders no one could hear.

The foreman's sorrel didn't help matters any, either. It pranced wildly, frightened by the din, on the verge of fleeing.

An idea occurred to Fargo and he took a gamble it would work. As the lanky cowboy roughly shoved Weaver up and over the saddle, Fargo raced to the front corner and fanned the Colt. Not at the cowhands, however. He shot at the ground in front of the sorrel and another spooked horse.

It was all the nudge they needed. Wheeling, both animals sped madly from the scene. Weaver had to cling to the sorrel's mane for dear life while the other puncher made a few half hearted tries at turning his chestnut and then gave it up.

The three remaining hands hardly hesitated. They snapped off a few more shots before applying their spurs and joining their companions in making themselves scarce.

Fargo felt no urge to gloat. Luck had saved him, nothing else. And it was only temporary. Those cowboys would flee for a few miles before coming to their senses. One would stay with Weaver while the rest rushed back loaded for bear, anxious to prove they weren't the cowards they had seemed to be. He had to be long gone by then.

Going into the line shack, Fargo rolled up his bedroll, shouldered his saddle, and jogged to the gully. He was out of breath when he got there, which was nothing compared to the shock which awaited him.

Jennifer Ragsdale was gone.

9

It became clear soon after Skye Fargo started tracking Jennifer Ragsdale that she was not heading for the Bar R. Her trail pointed to the northwest. Judging by the spacing of her mount's tracks and the depth of the prints, she had walked the animal for the first mile, stopping once, possibly when the shooting broke out, to turn and gaze toward the line shack. From there on she urged the mare at a gallop.

Fargo had underestimated her. He never would have left her alone if he had known she was strong enough to ride. Either she had recovered much more quickly than was normal, or she had been shamming to trick him. Either way, at the rate she was pushing herself she might have a relapse.

Head wounds were peculiar. No two ever had the same effect. One person might be struck a glancing blow and go on about his business as if nothing had happened. Another person, hit with the same amount of force, might need days in bed to recuperate and suffer bouts of dizziness and weakness for weeks or months on end.

Fargo had to glue his eyes to the ground to read the sign. So, hours later he glanced up sharply when a large shadow fell across the pinto, to find himself staring at the looming mouth of a rocky canyon. The tracks led straight into its depths.

Pulling the Sharps from the boot, Fargo rode on. The walls were high, the sides sheer in most places. He felt hemmed in and vulnerable and shifted constantly to scan the rims for riflemen. The canyon was so far off the beaten path that it would make an ideal sanctuary for someone wanted by the law. But the only set of hoofprints he had seen so far were those belonging to the tiring mare.

What business did Jennifer Ragsdale have in such a godforsaken place? Fargo reflected. A bend appeared so he slowed and leveled the rifle. Stopping shy of the turn, he craned his neck. A long, straight stretch broadened to form a hidden oasis of lush vegetation. Perhaps half a mile away smoke rose from a stand of trees.

Fargo checked the ground again. The only tracks he saw were those of Jennifer's horse, yet there had to be others back in there. And it wasn't hard to guess whose they were.

Rather than leave the Ovaro behind and risk it being found by a bandit, Fargo boldly rode on, hugging the base of the right-hand wall, the Sharps tucked to his shoulder so he could fire the instant a threat presented itself.

It was an ordeal, traveling the length of those stone walls to the green island beyond. Fargo figured the gang would have men posted on top of the canyon, and he never knew when one of them might pop up and blast away. He constantly swiveled right and left and back and forth. Once a pebble rattled down from on high, but when he looked all he saw was a lizard scuttling across a jagged outcropping.

At length Fargo came to where the canyon widened. His best guess was that the walls were over a mile apart. He was about to make for the nearest cover when a gust of hot air fanned his right cheek. Turning, he saw only solid rock. Yet the rush of air was stronger than ever.

Fargo moved closer and was amazed to discover a recessed niche big enough for a horse and rider to enter. Thinking it might be the opening to a cave, he advanced a few yards and saw that the niche was actually the end of a narrow winding passage which went clear through the canyon wall to the outside world. He also spied scores of tracks in the dirt, evidence the passage had been used many times by many men. It was a secret entrance used by the bandits.

Now Fargo understood how Maxwell had eluded search parties for so long. Anyone coming across the mouth of the canyon would have seen there were no tracks and passed it by. Odds were, the secret, true entrance was well hidden and that the bandits took great pains to erase any tracks leading to it.

Moving back out into the open, Fargo trotted into the trees. Hardly had he gained cover than voices wafted to his ears. Well screened by the brush, he watched a clearly defined trail and shortly was rewarded by the sight of two men in sombreros. They were in fine spirits, laughing as they went by within sixty feet of his hiding place. Into the niche they rode, and for a while Fargo could hear the ghostly echoes of their muffled voices.

Fargo let them go because it was Maxwell he wanted, and gunfire would forewarn the butcher. Santiago, after all, was the leader, the one who had organized the gang. If Maxwell were to be put behind bars or killed, the gang might fall apart.

Picking his way with care, Fargo walked the stallion toward the smoke. It was ironic that the very mistake which had led Bo Weaver to the line shack was leading Fargo to his quarry. He suspected that the *bandidos* had grown too sure of themselves and were beginning to believe the tall tales told about them. They didn't think anyone could find them, so they had grown sloppy.

It was a blunder they would regret.

In order to prevent any of the gang's mounts from picking up the Ovaro's scent, Fargo reined up among some junipers, ground-hitched the stallion, and continued on foot. When he heard more voices, he glided along in a crouch. When the outline of a building appeared through the trees, he sank even lower. The final dozen yards, he crawled.

From under a scrub oak Fargo laid eyes on the bandit stronghold. It had been wisely chosen. A large spring afforded plenty of water. There was ample grass for forage. And a steep cliff cast cool shade over a crudely built cabin even smaller than the line shack.

Fargo counted eight bandits but there had to be more inside since fourteen horses were grazing nearby. Of the eight, six appeared to be half-breeds of one kind or another. Another was Mexican, the last a full-blooded Navaho well on in years. All were heavily armed. Most wore two pistols and a Bowie or other big knife. Most had bandoliers crisscrossing their chests, the loops glistening thick with cartridges. And every one of them except the Navaho wore a sombrero.

Fargo rested his chin on his wrist and studied the horses. Jennifer's mare wasn't among them. Yet she had to be there. He pulled his hat brim low against the harsh glare of sunlight and bided his time.

For the longest while nothing happened. The bandits sat in the shade, drinking, cursing, and joking. Two of them held a knife-throwing contest, using a knot in a tree as a target. The loser forked over some money.

Suddenly Fargo realized the Navaho was gone. On the off chance the warrior had spotted him, Fargo surveyed the area, without result. He was about to snake back into the brush to see if the Navaho had circled around and was creeping up on him from behind when a commotion erupted in a thicket to the east. Instantly the bandits flashed their pistols out. The brush parted to reveal the aged warrior with a struggling captive.

It was Jennifer Ragsdale.

The cutthroats converged at a run but halted at a bellow from the cabin. In the doorway stood Santiago Maxwell. Scowling, he moved toward the Navaho, five other bandits filing out of the cabin in his wake. Several were yawning or tucking in shirts.

Fargo took advantage of the distraction and moved closer, to a boulder. When he peeked out, he saw that Santiago had Jennifer by the arm and was hauling her toward the cabin. Several *bandidos* laughed but fell silent when he glared at them.

Jennifer was tugging her arm, trying to break loose. She dug in her heels, then cried out, "Max, stop this! You're hurting me!"

Santiago let go and faced her. His handsome, hawkish features were curled in flinty resentment. "How do you know about this place?" he growled.

His tone caused Jennifer to recoil. "I followed you once, that time we met at the shack and I warned you about Pa organizing the ranchers to track you down. Remember?"

A string of foul words in Spanish gushed from Maxwell before he reverted to English. "I was careless. It will never hap-pen again." His hand flicked out like a striking snake and he gripped the front of her dress. "Why did you come?" he probed. "Did you lead Skye Fargo here?"

"No. Never."

"Bitch!" Maxwell roared, shaking her as a wolf might shake its prey. "Do you expect me to take your word for it? After you led me into a trap?"

"I didn't—," Jennifer began, and was roughly shoved to the ground. She was more upset than scared. As tears filled her eyes, she held out a hand, imploring, and said, "How could you think I would do such a thing? And how can you treat me like this? Doesn't our love mean anything to you anymore?"

"Love!" Santiago practically screamed. The crack of his hand slapping her cheek like the crack of a whip. "When will you get it through that stupid head of yours that I do not love you? Whatever we had between us is over. It died the day your father put the lash to my back."

Jennifer went to rise. "You can't mean that!"

Beside himself with fury, Maxwell seized her and slapped her again and again and again. He would have kept on hitting her had the Navaho not bounded up and gripped his arm.

"No more!" the warrior said in the tongue of his people.

Maxwell glared but relented. He tossed Jennifer down like a pile of discarded rags and straddled her. Her face was as red as a beet and she was woozy from the beating but she managed to raise her head.

"How could you, my love?"

"I am not your lover!" Maxwell said, shaking a fist at her. "You are so blind that you cannot see the truth!" He kicked her in the side. "Listen, and know the truth at last." Maxwell had to take a breath to steady himself. "Why do you think I came to see you five months ago, after so much time had passed? Because I missed you and couldn't stand to be away from you?"

Jennifer, dazed, nodded.

"Wrong! I knew I could get you to spy on your father for me and to report all that you heard. I tricked you into being my

101

eyes and my ears so I could stay one step ahead of the gringo pigs who want me dead."

"No!" Jennifer said in a pathetic whine.

"Yes, bitch! I used you." The butcher laughed, a high, dry crackle. "Think of it! I would like to see the look on your father's face when he learns what I have done. And he will. I will see to it." He drew back a boot to kick her again but changed his mind. "I will have the last laugh, Jenny. I will show all of them."

Fargo cocked the Sharps and inched to the edge of the boulder. Other than the Navaho, the bandits were standing in a group, watching their leader. He had them right where he wanted them, all in one spot. Pressing the smooth stock to his shoulder, he took aim at Maxwell's chest. But just as he did, the Navaho stepped into his line of fire to help Jennifer rise. She clung to the warrior, drained of all strength.

Fargo couldn't shoot until she was in the clear. The Navaho made no move, though, to escort her away. The warrior said something to Santiago, who shook his head and turned to the Mexican

"Take her inside, Alfredo. Tie her well. We will make use of her tomorrow."

Fargo couldn't let her out of his sight. There was no telling what might happen. Once he opened fire, one of the cutthroats might kill her for the sheer hell of it. So, taking the bull by the horns in a manner of speaking, he sprang into the open, moving several strides from the boulder to allow for an unobstructed shot at Santiago Maxwell. Then, taking a bead, he called out, "No one move!"

Most of the bandits froze, bewildered. But not Maxwell, who grinned slyly and slowly hooked his thumbs in his gunbelt. Nor did the Navaho show any alarm. The warrior simply stared and frowned.

"Well, well, well," Maxwell declared. "What do we have here? The hired gringo killer playing hero?" He looked at Jennifer in withering contempt. "So you didn't bring Fargo? Isn't that what you claimed, you lying *puta*?"

Fargo took a few steps toward them to better see the hands

of those clustered at the middle of the pack. "I shadowed her," he said. "She never knew I was there."

Santiago chuckled in scorn. "And jackasses have wings and can fly." Gesturing defiantly, he said, "Put down the rifle, gringo, and I will be generous. I will kill you outright instead of piece by gory piece."

"I'm the one who has you in his sights," Fargo pointed out, "not the other way around."

"*Sí*, you do, but there are fifteen of us and only one of you. The moment you squeeze that trigger, my men will shoot you to ribbons." Maxwell puffed out his chest. "Go ahead. Prove me wrong. Fire if you dare."

It was the sort of challenge only someone who didn't care to live would make, and it was all the more galling because Fargo realized the renegade had him between a rock and a hard place. There was no way Fargo could outgun fourteen *pistoleros* and a Navaho warrior in a standup gunfight.

"I am waiting," Maxwell taunted. "What is taking you so long to make up your mind? Perhaps you need some help, eh?" Whipping out a Bowie, he sidled toward Jennifer. "What if I stab this foolish one? Will that be enough to make you act?"

Fargo wished Jennifer would come to her senses and bolt, but she stood there as meekly as a lamb being led to the slaughter, her expression as blank as a chalk slate. The Mexican, Alfredo, had released her, freeing his gun hand.

"You disappoint me, gringo," Maxwell said with a sigh. "Truly, you do. I was told you are formidable, but now I see you are as yellow as all gringos. You are only brave when your enemies are tied to fence rails and can not fight back."

"I'm not William Ragsdale," Fargo said, and did exactly what they didn't think he would do. He shot Santiago Maxwell. Or he tried to, but at the very split second that he fired, Alfredo lunged to one side and drew. The Mexican thought he had an edge, thought he could put a slug into Fargo before Fargo made up his mind, but he blundered directly in front of Maxwell and took the slug meant for the leader. The impact hurled him into Santiago and they both crashed to the ground.

Since Fargo couldn't hope to outgun the gang, he had decided to lure them away from Jennifer and sneak back to get her. No sooner did he fire than he spun and raced toward the horses. He covered ten feet before the bandits belatedly came to life, and suddenly the canyon walls echoed to the thunder of a dozen guns blazing away at once. The earth around him spewed dirt. At any moment he expected to feel a searing pain in his back but he reached the animals without being so much as nicked.

"Don't fire! Don't fire! You'll hit our horses!" someone frantically yelled above the booming guns as Fargo weaved in among the startled mounts. A few still grazed unconcerned, but the majority nickered and pranced in rising panic. He skirted a zebra dun and heard bullets thud into it. The horse squealed in agony.

"Damn it, stop firing and go get him!" Maxwell roared. "I want the bastard alive so I can make him suffer as he has never suffered before."

Fargo looked back over the shoulders of a paint. The bandits were rushing in pursuit. Drawing the Colt, he snapped a shot at the fleetest and the half-breed clutched at his torso and fell. It slowed the others down, enabling him to dash to the far side of the milling animals. The horses yearned to flee but were held by tethers fastened to picket pins, a prudent precaution in Apache country.

Dropping low, Fargo sprinted behind the small cabin. The bandits had fanned out and were among the horses. None had noticed his change of direction. Keeping the cabin between him and them, he worked around to the south wall. From here he could see Alfredo lying in a spreading red puddle. Beside the body stood Jennifer, her head bowed. There was no sign of Santiago Maxwell.

Fargo moved to the front corner. Maxwell had gone several yards nearer to the horses and was telling his men to spread out even more and leave no stone unturned. The bandit had his back to Jennifer—and to Fargo.

Girding himself, Fargo bolted to the woman's side. All would have been well had she stayed in her benumbed state for a little bit longer. But she saw Fargo and snapped erect, rousing to life at the worst possible moment.

"Skye! I knew you wouldn't desert me!"

At her outburst, Santiago Maxwell swung around, his hands stabbing at his revolvers. The renegade was fast, but Fargo already had the Colt out and only had to stroke the trigger. He wanted to fill the butcher with lead but he had to fire on the fly and contented himself with seeing the side of Maxwell's head explode in a shower of blood.

Grabbing Jennifer's hand, Fargo fled to the south. Shouts filled the air behind the cabin. A man called Santiago's name over and over. Fargo set his eyes on the thicket and increased the length of his stride. He assumed the blonde would keep up with him but she foiled him by tripping over her own feet and doing an ungainly dive. His arm was nearly torn out of its socket but he held on to her hand.

"Get up!" Fargo prompted, pulling her erect. "And if you value your life, run like hell."

Jennifer gulped and nodded. They raced into the vegetation as bullets buzzed and zinged around them. Fargo veered to the right, went fifty yards, then veered to the left. They passed a large slab of rock tilted at an angle. Digging in his heels, Fargo darted back to it and dropped onto his hands and knees. There was barely enough space for a person to lie flat.

"Crawl on in."

"What?" Jennifer responded. "Under there? Wouldn't it be smarter to keep on running? There might be snakes or scorpions."

"Would you rather be bit or shot?" Fargo said, and pushed her, hard. She fearfully obeyed, turning so she faced the opening and eased in on her left side. Fargo immediately rolled onto his back and squeezed in beside her, forcing her to go farther when she balked.

Footsteps drummed. The bandits were close.

"Oh, God," Jennifer whispered. "I can feel something squiggling against my leg. We have to get out of here."

"No time," Fargo said curtly, molding himself to her from head to toe. Shoving, he crammed her back against the slab.

Her face brushed his. Her mouth was the width of a hair from his own.

"I don't like this."

"Quiet!"

The footsteps were so close Fargo could feel the vibrations through the ground. Twisting his neck, he saw a succession of boots fly past the boulder. Spurs jingled. Dust flew. Fargo felt an urge to sneeze and exerted all his will to keep from giving their location away.

The bandits were soon out of sight. Gradually the dust settled. The shouts died.

"Shouldn't we go while we can?" Jennifer whispered, her breath warm on his cheek.

"Not yet," Fargo said, wanting to be sure the cutthroats were long gone. He shifted to see her face and by accident their mouths touched. She drew back, or tried to. She was wedged so tight there was no room. "Sorry," he said.

"Think nothing of it," Jennifer said. "And while I have the chance, I want to thank you for saving my life. Max would have killed me if you hadn't come along. I never thought he could do such a thing, but I was wrong. So terribly, stupidly wrong." She bit her lip. "He's not the same man I loved. Not by a long shot."

Fargo went to shrug but it was too cramped. "People change," he said softly. "Sometimes they change for the worse." He thought he heard a noise. When he felt it was safe, he asked, "Where's your mare?"

"I left her back a ways. I can't say exactly how far, but I walked for five minutes before I saw the cabin."

By Fargo's reckoning that meant that the mare was near the tree line. The horse would be safe for the time being. But they had to move fast to get there before the bandits came across it. "Come on," he said, clasping her hand.

Grunting and wriggling, Fargo slid out from underneath the massive boulder. He tried not to think of what would have happened if the boulder had fallen flat while they were under it. Jennifer squirmed out beside him, then stopped. Her dress had snagged. She attempted to yank it loose without tearing it.

"There's no time for this," Fargo complained, swinging her to her feet. She was none too happy when the fabric tore from her hem halfway to her waist.

Fargo headed in the general direction of the Ovaro. He moved quietly as a panther, avoiding twigs and dry leaves. Jennifer, however, had an uncanny knack for stepping on every one in their path. After going only twenty feet, he bent to her ear and said, "Watch my feet. Step exactly where I do." From then on she did fine.

All things considered, Fargo mused, everything had turned out for the best. He had saved Jennifer. Santiago Maxwell was dead. Now he could continue to Las Cruces and put the Socorro slaughter behind him.

In due course the stallion appeared. Eager to reach it, Fargo forged ahead without noticing that the pinto's head was held high and it was staring intently at a nearby bush. He understood why when he went to take hold of the reins.

Uttering a war whoop, the Navaho warrior leaped out at them.

10

The warrior had a gleaming knife held overhead. Although on in years, his muscles were supple and strong. His speed was the equal of a man half his age, and by all rights he should have buried his blade in Fargo. He was in midair when Jennifer Ragsdale let out a shriek of sheer terror that would have done justice to a banshee. The Navaho glanced at her, taking his eyes off Fargo for no more than a few heartbeats. But it was enough.

Skye Fargo had reflexes most men would envy. A lifetime of living on the raw frontier, where often whether a man lived or died depended on how quick he was, had honed his body to a razor edge. As the warrior hurtled toward him, he grabbed the Sharps with both hands and drove the stock into the Navaho's gut.

The warrior was slammed head over heels and dumped in the grass on his shoulders. Stunned, he rolled onto his stomach and put both hands flat to push to his feet.

Fargo took aim at the back of the warrior's head and had his thumb on the hammer when Jennifer unexpectedly jumped in front of him and shoved the barrel to one side.

"Don't kill him! Please! He helped me back there."

Fargo couldn't see the Navaho. Dreading that the warrior was pulling a pistol, he gave the blonde a push and took a short step to the left in case the renegade opened fire. But the man was just sitting there, his bronzed hands over his stomach. The knife lay a few feet from him.

"No one has ever hit me so hard, white man," the Navaho said in clipped English between ragged breaths. "You must be as strong as a bear."

The man made no move to use his revolvers but Fargo was taking no chances. Plucking them from their holsters, he threw them into the brush, then did the same with the knife. "You can give thanks to Earth Mother," he said, referring to one of the holy people to whom the tribe prayed. "You get to live if you sit there and behave yourself."

Fargo motioned for Jennifer to mount. "Hurry it up. The bandits might have heard that scream of yours."

Ignoring him, she rested a hand on the Navaho's shoulder and said, "I want to thank you for what you did. It was very brave of you to stop Max from hitting me."

"Not so brave," the warrior said. "Santiago would never hurt me."

"He'd hurt anyone," Jennifer said. "Trust me. I know that better than anyone."

"Not me," the Navaho insisted. "I am his grandfather."

Fargo stared at him. There was no family resemblance that he could see unless it was in the dark eyes. But where Maxwell's eyes were pools of hatred, the warrior's hinted at a kinder disposition.

Jennifer wagged a finger. "You should be ashamed of yourself. A man your age, riding with a band of killers. How could you?" she scolded.

To Fargo's surprise, the Navaho didn't laugh in her face. While not as notorious as Apaches, the Navahos had done their fair share of making life miserable for Mexican and American settlers for years. They had raided countless ranches and haciendas and slaughtered scores of men, women, and children.

"I thought I could make him stop," the old man said forlornly, "but I was wrong. When I saw him hitting you, Golden Hair, I knew he would never change." The warrior looked at Fargo. "I am called Coyote, white man. I am tired of this life, and I ask that you take me with you."

The old man's request was so strange that Fargo suspected Coyote of deliberately delaying them. So far there was no trace of the bandits but they might show up at any moment. Fargo wanted to mount up and get out of there. "If you aim to split with your grandson, then do it. You don't need us." He prodded Jennifer with his hand. "Get on the Ovaro while we still can."

Reluctantly, she did so. Fargo swung up behind her, hooked an arm around her waist, and lifted the reins. Then something yanked on his pant leg.

"I speak with a straight tongue, white man. I want to go with you."

The last thing Fargo needed was for the warrior to tag along. It might be a trick. Coyote would contrive to slow them down or else might leave secret signs so the bandits could follow them. "Afraid not. You're on your own," he said.

Jennifer shifted. "Oh, let him come! What harm can he do unarmed? I'll keep my eyes on him if it will make you feel safer."

Saying nothing, Fargo clucked the stallion forward. They had wasted enough time. If the warrior wanted to tag along, he was welcome to. All he had to do was keep up.

It was slow-going at first. Fargo held the Ovaro to a walk to reduce the noise they made. He avoided open spaces and stopped frequently to listen. All the while, Coyote jogged at the stallion's side.

The warrior was the first to spy the mare. Pointing, he declared, "There is another horse."

"Mine," Jennifer revealed.

For her to switch mounts took hardly any time. Fargo scanned behind them, unable to understand why the *bandidos* weren't hard on their heels. Staying close to the tree line, he rode to the west wall and along it to the point where the canyon narrowed. He found the secret niche with no trouble and took the narrow passage to the rim.

The cabin was so well hidden among the trees that Fargo couldn't pinpoint it, nor did he see any of the bandits. It was unlikely that the killers had given up, that they wouldn't try to avenge the deaths of their three dead, yet such seemed to be the case. He wheeled the Ovaro to leave and heard Jennifer's saddle creak. She had given the warrior a hand up behind her. "What do you think you're doing?" Fargo asked.

110

"Coyote can't keep up on foot."

The old warrior grinned at Fargo, who didn't bother to return the favor. The Navaho had yet to persuade him that he was sincere. Lightly applying his spurs, he galloped due west. The Bar R lay to the south, which was the direction the bandits would expect them to take. By swinging westward, he hoped to avoid another clash.

They were abroad during the worst heat of the day. Soon riders and animals were slick with sweat and the mare was showing signs of going lame. Fargo reined up to examine her legs but found nothing wrong other than that she was overweight from lack of exercise. It was a sad fact of life that many people pampered their horses, never realizing that they slashed years off the animal's life.

Pushing on, Fargo reached the plains of San Augustin as twilight descended. Rather than head south then and there, he turned north into a range of low hills and eventually called a halt in a clearing among pinion trees. "We'll make a cold camp," he announced.

"No fire?" Jennifer said. "No coffee or hot food? I haven't eaten a decent meal since I left the ranch. I'm famished."

Fargo took jerky from his saddlebags. "This will have to hold you until you're safely home." He offered a piece to her but she shook her head.

"I never have been fond of jerked meat. It's too salty for my taste."

"It's better than an empty belly." Fargo saw the Navaho eyeing the handful hungrily and gave the warrior some. Coyote tore into his share as if he hadn't eaten in a month of Sundays. They sat in a circle, Jennifer close to Fargo, both of them with their backs to a low log. The darkness deepened, and soon they could barely see the horses even though the animals were twenty feet away.

Fargo finished his jerky, folded his arms, and leaned back. It had been a rough two days and he could use a good night's sleep, but he had to stay awake and keep an eye on the Navaho.

Coyote's face was in shadow. He cleared his throat, then

said, "I know what you are thinking, white man, but I will do you no harm. I am not like my grandson."

"You were part of his gang," Fargo said bluntly. "And you were the one who dragged Miss Ragsdale into their camp."

"I did so to keep her from being shot. She was making more noise than a herd of horses, and I heard her long before the others. If one of them had seen her first, she would be dead." Coyote paused. "As for riding with Santiago, I thought I could talk him out of his evil ways. He always listened to my words when he was younger. But twelve moons ago something happened to him. Now he never listens to me. He calls me an old fool to my face."

Jennifer shook her head in dismay. "Oh, you poor dear, to be put through that kind of ordeal. My heart goes out to you, Coyote. We've both been hurt by Max, and I, for one, will never be the same."

"He told me about you," Coyote said. "For a while, when the two of you were very close, he was the happiest I have ever seen him. He even forgot about his mother and father."

Despite himself, Fargo wanted to learn more. "How do you mean?" he asked. "What happened to them?"

The Navaho seemed to withdraw within himself. His voice had a haunted aspect when he answered. "They died too young. Not from sickness. No, hatred killed both of them. Hatred of them because they had mixed blood." He made a teepee of his fingers. "Santiago's father, my son, wanted to live in peace with everyone. He never struck another person in his life, a trait he got from his mother. She was Mexican, a captive I took when I was young and did not know any better. And because my son was a breed, my people wanted little to do with him."

"And Max's mother?" Jennifer inquired.

"She was a sweet woman, a great wife. But her tender heart could not take it when the other whites shunned her for taking up with my son." Coyote placed a hand to his brow. "One day Santiago's father was found dead, stabbed in the back. No one knows who did it, but I have heard talk, rumors that some of our warriors killed him for daring to live with a white-eye. His wife did not last long after he died. She sat in her chair, wasting away to nothing, and one day just stopped breathing."

"Poor Santiago," Jennifer said. "He never told me, but I suspected as much."

Fargo was silent, thinking. He saw now that the whipping Ragsdale had given Maxwell was the straw that broke the camel's back. Santiago had tried hard to live by the same code as his folks, and look at what it had got him. Small wonder he had turned renegade and was killing every white he set eyes on. From what he had seen in the canyon, Santiago Maxwell was near insane with rage and a thirst for vengeance.

In a short while Jennifer and Coyote turned in. Fargo stood and prowled the vicinity. An owl hooted to the southwest and a mountain lion screamed far to the north. Otherwise, the woodland was quiet.

Convinced it would be safe to get some badly needed rest, Fargo walked back to the log and was lowering himself to the ground when he discovered the Navaho was missing. Shooting erect, he scoured the clearing. The horses were still there, grazing by the trees. He glanced down to see if the Sharps had been stolen but it was right where he had left it, propped on his saddle.

Even so, Fargo was uneasy. The Navahos were known to be extremely clever. Coyote might have played on their sympathies so they would let down their guard. He gave the old man a full ten minutes to show himself, then gently nudged Jennifer's arm. "Wake up. We might have trouble." All she did was mumble and smack her lips so he shook her until she whipped up off the grass.

"What is it? What's the matter?"

"We have to go. The Navaho is missing. He might have gone to get the others and lead them to us."

"What?" Jennifer ran a hand through her hair. "I don't believe that for a minute. Coyote is too nice a man. I'm sure there must be a perfectly good explanation."

"We're not waiting around to find out."

Fargo saddled both horses. Jennifer objected but he insisted she climb on. "Stay close," he cautioned, slanting to the northeast. There was no moon so it was as black as tar and the brush was nearly as thick. He lost count of the number of branches that snagged his buckskins or nicked his face and hands. In order not to give them away, he rode at a snail's pace. In an hour they covered not quite half a mile.

From there on, Fargo pushed the horses as fast as was practical. Presently, quite by chance, they came on a stream no more than ankle deep. If the rains didn't arrive soon, it would dry up. Fargo watered the horses, tethered both, and joined Jennifer on the grassy bank. He spread out his blankets, claimed half for himself, then lay down. "You can do the same," he said. "We've given them the slip."

"Thanks to you." Jennifer sat, her arms draped over her knees. "I owe you more than I can ever repay. You've gone to a lot of trouble on my behalf even though I've given you a hard time every step of the way. Why?"

"It had to be done," Fargo said, closing his eyes and wishing she would hush up so he could doze off. She had hardly said two words since they left the first camp, yet now she wanted to talk. As usual, her timing was rotten.

"But you don't know me that well. You risked your life for a near stranger. I'd say that's very noble of you."

Fargo cracked an eye. "Don't go making me out to be more than I am."

"And what exactly are you?"

"A man who wants you to shut up so he can get some sleep." Rolling onto his side so his back was to her, Fargo curled his arms at his chest and let himself drift off. They had to get an early start and would be in the saddle most of the day. He wouldn't get more than four hours of rest. Maybe less.

A hand touched his shoulder.

Fargo opened both eyes. He heard Jennifer sliding toward him, felt her body lie flush against his. Her hand crept to his neck and stroked gently. "Just what the hell do you think you're doing?" he asked.

"It should be as plain as the nose on your face," she answered huskily.

Sighing, Fargo rolled back onto his back. "I'm a near stranger, remember? And it must be two in the morning."

Jennifer propped herself on his chest and toyed with his hair, a seductive grin inviting him to do as he pleased. "So what? I've heard that men are always in the mood, no matter what time it is."

"Little girls shouldn't believe everything they hear," Fargo grumbled, giving her a push which she resisted.

"In case you haven't noticed, I'm not a little girl," Jennifer said. "Some say I'm almost as beautiful as my sister, although I don't believe them."

"You're better-looking than she is," Fargo made the mistake of saying, and the next moment soft, moist lips smothered his and a tongue as glassy as silk delved deep into his mouth. He responded, but more out of habit than desire. When she broke for air, she smirked and tweaked his ear.

"As that crusty old book my pa likes to read says, I think you protest too much. You say one thing but your mouth says something else."

"My mouth isn't as tired as the rest of me," Fargo told her. Any other time or place and he would have been all over her like a bear on honey. But he knew that if he didn't catch up on his sleep, he would pay for it the next day.

"My brave protector," Jennifer said with a smidgen of sarcasm. "You'll go up against a whole gang of hardened killers just to save me, but you're afraid to let your true feelings show."

"I don't have any feelings for you."

"Come now. You can be honest with me. I know why you've gone to so much trouble. Secretly, you care for me as much as I once cared for Max."

That did it. Fargo decided she was about ten cards shy of a full deck. Then he thought back to other women he had bailed out of tight spots and recalled how grateful many of them had been. Maybe it was something in human nature that made helpless victims look on those who saved them as being special. Jennifer simply had added a new twist. She mistook simple concern for love.

"You're wrong," Fargo said.

"Am I? I know how to prove it."

Fargo opened his mouth to ask how, and she swooped her lips to his to give him a repeat of the first kiss, only this one lasted longer and her hands roamed over his body the whole while. Her fingers massaged his stomach, straying lower but stopping short of his manhood, which was growing harder by the second.

Suddenly Fargo no longer wanted or needed sleep. He craved something else. She had only herself to blame for being so insistent.

"Listen," Fargo said when she pulled back, "I'm trying to be honest with you. I like you, but not the way you think. And if we make love, it will be because *you* want to."

Jennifer made no reply for almost a minute. "Fair enough, Skye Fargo. You don't love me. And maybe I don't love you. But I do care, an awful lot. And I want you in a way I've never wanted any man except Max. Do you understand?" She leaned down and kissed him again, her hands going to his cheeks, his ears, his hair.

It was as if she were starving and Fargo was a full course meal. She kissed and nibbled and licked him all over, unfastening his shirt as she did, her mouth and hands arousing him to a fever pitch.

Fargo's organ throbbed. He pulled her face to his and locked his mouth on hers. His hands found the buttons and catches to her dress. As her wonderful mounds were bared and his fingers pinched her nipples, she sucked in her breath and arched her back. Fargo raised his lips to her right breast and sucked, rubbing both as he did. It drove her wild.

For someone who had not had much experience with men, Jennifer Ragsdale knew just what to do and how to respond to every caress. Together they stroked the flames of raw lust. It was difficult to say which of them became more excited but not to tell which was more vocal. Jennifer cooed and moaned and cried out now and then.

Fargo flipped her onto her back. Parting her legs, he reached up under dress, stroking her smooth skin, going higher and higher. Her thighs quivered as he ran his hand over them. His fingers came to her core and found her volcanic, ready to explode. Yet Fargo wasn't ready. She had started it; he was going to finish it when he was good and ready.

Sliding a finger to her slit, Fargo suddenly thrust it in to the knuckle. Jennifer said his name and bucked against him in wild abandon. It was all he could do to hold her down as he pumped his finger. She entwined her slender fingers behind his head and mashed his face to hers, greedily kissing him as if there would be no tomorrow.

With his free hand Fargo hitched her dress to her waist. He inserted a second finger into her innermost recesses, which added to her pleasure and made her toss her head from side to side while she groaned as if at death's door. He lathered her breasts, then licked lower, tracing the outline of a rib with his tongue.

"I never knew!" Jennifer breathed.

Fargo had no idea what she meant and he wasn't about to spoil the moment by asking. He reached under her to cup her tight bottom and add leverage to his finger thrusts. Her knees bent and she pulled him between them, her urgency mounting. But still he held off.

Kneeling, Fargo undid his pants to expose his pole. He pulled out his fingers and rubbed the tip of himself against her, showing her that the best was yet to come. She glanced down, then took him unawares by wrapping her hand around his member. Her body was giving off more heat than a campfire and her eyes seemed to glow.

Jennifer pulled him down on top of her so she could explore his mouth with her tongue while her hand explored his pole from end to end. It was an exquisite feeling and Fargo nearly lost control. Rising up, he placed his hands on her heaving melons. Her hips rose off the ground and she ground herself into him, trying to entice him to put his organ where his fingers had been.

Pushing her thighs wide, Fargo positioned himself. He fed his member in slowly, savoring the tingle which coursed up his spine. She was in a rapture of her own, her rosy lips parted, her head bent back, her gaze fixed on the stars.

At Fargo's first stroke, Jennifer rose to meet him, her arms clinging to his back, her nails digging into his flesh. Their mouths fused. They were one from head to toe, one in the rhythms of their entwined bodies, one in the pulsing, driving urgency which made them go ever faster until they were rocking in the flush of unbridled passion.

Jennifer went over the edge first. Her nails dug deeper. Her back nearly bent in half. And from the depths of her being issued a wavering moan which was borne off on the night breeze. Then her bottom pumped madly and her inner walls closed around him.

For his part, Fargo had held back as long as he could. He let himself go and they pounded into one another. Her breasts cushioned his chest, her hips braced his thighs. Their hearts beat to the same drum. In unison they reached the crest and coasted on waves of sensual pleasure. Then, ever so gradually, they slowed.

Fargo, totally spent, rolled off her. He tried to stay awake but his eyes closed of their own accord and at long last he got his wish. He fell asleep, the last sound he heard that of something moving nearby.

One of the horses, Fargo figured.

11

Skye Fargo came awake slowly. Warmth on his face told him he had overslept, that the sun was already up. Feeling drowsy, he was about to drift off again when he had the distinct impression that someone was watching him. Assuming it to be Jennifer Ragsdale, he opened his eyes.

The blonde lay at his side, curled in a ball, sound asleep.

Twisting, Fargo checked on the horses. They were fine. He lifted his arms to stretch, then froze. Seated eight feet away was the old warrior, Coyote the Navaho, and the man held Fargo's Sharps trained squarely on Fargo's chest. Tucked under the warrior's belt was Fargo's own Colt.

"Good morning, white-eyes. I trust you had a good sleep. You slept very soundly."

Fargo lowered his arms and sat up. His buckskins were still in disarray, his pants down near his knees. He quickly dressed, thankful he had left his boots on. The warrior had overlooked the toothpick, which Fargo was going to bury in the treacherous Indian's throat the first chance he got.

"It is not wise for a man to sleep so soundly," Coyote went on. "You never know when an enemy will find you."

Irritated at having his nose rubbed in it, Fargo said, "Gloat all you want, Navaho. Now I know you're just as bad as that loco grandson of yours."

Coyote's seamed face formed twice as many wrinkles. He looked at the Sharps, then smiled. "Oh. This. It is not what you think, white-eye."

Their voices woke up Jennifer. She sighed in contentment and opened her languid eyes. "Good morning," she said to Fargo. She didn't seem to notice his scowl and turned to the warrior. On seeing the rifle, she gasped. "Coyote, whatever is the meaning of this?"

The Navaho nodded at her. "Maybe you would like to dress first. I know white women are very fussy about such things."

Only then did Jennifer realize most of her charms were exposed to the world. Crimson colored her cheeks as she shifted so her back was to the warrior. Her fingers flew.

Fargo glanced at the Ovaro. He couldn't blame the stallion for not warning him when the Indian came back. It had seen them together. It knew the Navaho's scent. "So what's it going to be?" he asked. "Do you kill us outright, or do you take us to the canyon so the gang can finish us off?"

Coyote grinned slyly. "Nothing like that. If I wanted those bad men to get the two of you, I would not have gone off last night to hide our trail so they can not find us."

Confused, Fargo said, "If you're on our side, why did you take my guns?"

"I am not on your side, white man," the warrior said. "I look out for my own interests. And it is best for me if you leave this country. You shot my grandson. You have done what you came to do. Now I want you to go far away and never come back."

"I was fixing to do that anyway," Fargo said. "Give me my guns back and I'll light a shuck for Las Cruces."

The corners of the Navaho's mouth turned down. "I am sorry. I would like to do as you ask but I can not." He slowly stood. "There is no time to waste. Please be so kind as to saddle your horse and leave."

Fargo's confusion was growing. He couldn't believe the warrior was simply going to let him ride away. Coyote must have a secret motive, he reasoned. "What about Miss Ragsdale? I'm not leaving without her."

"She will be safe. I give you my word."

Jennifer was fully dressed. She chimed in with, "Here I thought you were such a nice man! What do you intend to do with me?"

Coyote moved to the left a few feet, nearer to the horses. "I will take you to your father. By tonight you will sleep in your own house." He smiled to reassure her. "You would do well to get on with your life, missy. Forget about my grandson. Forget you ever knew him."

Fargo rose into a crouch, gauging the distance to the warrior. It was too far to try anything. Yet. He straightened, taking a casual stride closer. Instantly the Navaho hefted the rifle, pointing the barrel at his belly. "I would not try it, white man. I know how to use a Sharps. At this range I can not miss. And even if I only wound you, your rifle will put a hole in you the size of a melon."

It was no exaggeration. Fargo picked up his saddle and saddle blanket and went to the Ovaro. Out of the corner of his eyes he watched Coyote but the wily warrior never let down his guard. When he had tightened the cinch, he walked back and rolled up his bedroll. Jennifer nervously watched his every move. He knew that she didn't want him to leave and he didn't blame her. Every word the Navaho had said might be a lie. He toted the bedroll and his saddlebags to the stallion and tied them on.

"Now you will get on and go," Coyote said.

Fargo turned. "No, I won't. I'm not leaving Miss Ragsdale here by herself."

"But I am with her," Coyote said, then blinked as understanding dawned. He almost appeared hurt that they would doubt him. "Heed my words, white-eye. I have no wish to harm the pretty one. I stopped going on the warpath long ago. As for women, I had to give them up after I saw eighty-five winters. Missy will be safe with me. I will not let her out of my sight until she is back with her family."

The warrior acted sincere but Fargo wasn't ready to give him the benefit of the doubt. "I'd like to believe you, Coyote. But I can't go."

The Navaho raised the rifle to his shoulder. "You have no choice. Leave now, or I will shoot you in the leg and throw you on your horse."

Jennifer jumped up and dashed over to Fargo, frantically waving her arms at Coyote. "Don't shoot him! Please! I'll talk him into leaving if you'll just lower the rifle."

The warrior made no move to do as she wanted. "He must go," was his only comment.

"Do as he says, Skye," Jennifer pleaded. "I'll be all right. He must be telling the truth about not wanting to hurt us. After all, he could have shot us dead while we slept, yet he didn't."

Torn between his distrust of the cagey Navaho and his aversion to being shot, Fargo stayed right where he was. Only when he heard the click of the rifle's hammer did he nod at the blonde and say, "I'd best be going. Take care of yourself." He looked her in the eyes as he spoke, hoping she would divine by his expression that he had no intention of deserting her. He planned to stay close by and jump the Navaho when a chance presented itself.

"I will," Jennifer said, smiling bravely.

Fargo turned to the stallion and grabbed hold of the saddle horn. As he lifted his dusty boot to the stirrups, there was a rush of footsteps to his rear. Too late, he tried to spin. A hard object crashed into his skull. He could feel his legs buckling as the world went black. But he didn't pass entirely out, or so he believed. After what seemed like no more than a minute or two, he struggled back to consciousness, resisting the pain which racked his head.

Suddenly Fargo realized he was swaying in a familiar motion. Straightening, he was appalled to find himself astride the Ovaro, only *backward*. His wrists had been tied behind his back, his ankles were lashed securely by a rope running under the pinto. "Damn that tricky Indian," Fargo fumed. Bracing himself he strained with all his strength while furiously wriggling his hands. The rope, *his* rope apparently, was so tight he could barely move his wrists. The fingers were numb, which meant the circulation had been cut off. Pausing, he glanced down and discovered the Sharps in the boot and the Colt jammed into his saddlebag. "What the hell?"

Trying another tactic, Fargo moved his legs as far as he could, both to the front and the back, seeing how much play there was. Practically none, as it turned out. And the chafing of the rope on the Ovaro's belly made the stallion nicker in annoyance.

Fargo surveyed his surroundings. The pinto was bearing him due east. He guessed that the warrior had tied him on, then pointed the Ovaro toward Socorro and given it a whack on the rump. The countryside was unfamiliar. He had no idea how far he had gone. A glance at the sun showed he had been unconscious for at least two hours so he must have gone some distance.

Being trussed up was bad enough. Being trussed up in the middle of Apache country, where he might run into a roving band of Mescaleros at any time, made matters that much worse. And as if that wasn't enough to turn his hair gray, the rest of Maxwell's bandits were out there, somewhere. If they found him, he'd be tortured and left to rot. And there wasn't a thing he could do to defend himself.

The Ovaro was moving along a low ridge dotted with scrub trees and boulders. Fargo called out softly, "Whoa, boy," and was gratified when the animal stopped. Once again he worked at his wrists, grimacing when the rope bit into his flesh. Soon he had to give up. He was tearing his wrists badly yet was no closer to freeing himself.

Bending to the right as far as he could, Fargo saw the loop which held his ankle in place. The knot was as big as day and would be easy to untie if he had the use of his hands. He jerked his leg outward a few times but all he succeeded in doing was lancing pain up his leg.

Shifting, Fargo looked over a shoulder. The stallion was staring at him. It didn't seem to know what to make of the strange way he was riding and stamped a hoof a few times as if impatient for him to quit his shenanigans so they could go on about their business.

"Stand still, boy. Don't move," Fargo coaxed.

An idea came to him, a desperate means of getting loose. In order for it to work the pinto had to stay right where it was, and he honestly had no idea if it would. If the Ovaro spooked and galloped off, he would be pounded to death under its flailing hooves.

Fargo examined both sides of the stallion before making his move. On the left was a patch of brown grass which would cushion his fall somewhat, so he inched in that direction, moving his legs slowly so the rope wouldn't dig into the pinto. By gradual degrees he slid further and further to the left until he was perched on the very edge of the saddle. His left foot was under the Ovaro, his right was hiked halfway to the stirrup.

Again Fargo glanced around. The stallion still watched him closely. "Whoa, boy," he said softly in case it had a mind to move. Then, taking a breath, he let his body slip over the side. He fell slowly, the rope connecting his ankles serving as an anchor. He could see it rubbing the Ovaro's hide, see the hide rippling as the stallion whinnied in discomfort and took a step.

"Whoa!" Fargo shouted. To his relief, the horse obeyed. He was now nearly upside down, his hat in the grass, his legs bearing his weight. By squirming he lowered himself even more, until his shoulders rested on the ground. It took some of the strain off his legs but made his shoulders hurt like hell.

The next moment the Ovaro lurched into awkward motion. Fargo saw a large rock directly in front of him and jerked his head aside to keep from striking it.

"Whoa! Stop, big fella! Whoa!"

A few more steps, and the Ovaro listened. Fargo licked his lips, then let out the breath he didn't know he had been holding. By bending to the right he could see his boot. It was so close, yet it might as well be in the next territory. He arched his spine and surged upward but only rose as high as the pinto's belly. The boot, and the Arkansas toothpick, were well out of reach.

Fargo checked the ground. About ten feet in front of the Ovaro was a jagged spur of rock which might suit his purposes. Lifting his torso, he called out, "Go, boy, go!" while moving his legs as best he could. He expected the stallion to walk forward but it started to break into a trot.

Once more Fargo had to bellow, "Whoa! Whoa!" The pinto halted but past the jagged spur. Twisting, Fargo saw it a foot or so behind him. He extended his arms backward but he couldn't quite reach. Marshaling his energy, he pumped his legs and worked toward the rear of the Ovaro. The horse fidgeted so he talked to it quietly to calm it.

At last the spur was under him. Fargo applied the rope to the flinty rock and sawed. His shoulders bunched, he persisted until the pain was too great to bear.

Fargo went limp, relaxing his muscles. A few strands of the rope had parted, that was all. At the rate he was going, it would take him most of the day to cut himself loose.

Then the wind brought an unwelcome sound, the nicker of another horse somewhere down the ridge.

"Shhhhh," Fargo said so the Ovaro wouldn't answer. By raising his head he could see partway to the bottom. Nothing moved, not even a bird. It occurred to him that whoever was down there had heard the stallion a minute ago and was trying to find it. He had to free himself before that happened.

Redoubling his efforts, Fargo sawed and sawed, pushing the rope against the rock. He had a hard time controlling his strokes and the serrated edge bit into his arm every few strokes. Gritting his teeth, he worked at a frenzied pace. Sweat streaked his face, dampened his shirt.

The horse below whinnied again, louder and closer. The Ovaro looked down the slope and shifted its legs but stayed silent.

Fargo was in agony. His arms were sore, his shoulders screaming with pangs of torment every time he moved them. His eyes blurred due to the sweat trickling from his forehead. He couldn't see whether the rope was parting or not. It felt as if there were more slack but he couldn't be sure.

The faint clop of a hoof electrified Fargo to go faster. He heard another, and another, dull echoes made by two or three horses, maybe more.

His arms were a mass of pain from wrist to neck. He had been hanging upside down so long that his lungs craved air. Breathing in deep, he attacked the rock in renewed earnest, heedless of the drops of blood which flecked his skin and sleeve. The slack widened. Just when he thought his arms were at their limit and was ready to stop, the rope parted.

Fargo lunged upward and slipped his hand under his boot. He fumbled at the ankle sheath and out slid the knife. The

125

blade made short shrift of the rope binding his ankles. He fell, his right shoulder bearing the brunt of the fall.

Moving out from under the Ovaro, Fargo stood. He spied his hat and ran to reclaim it. As he wedged it on his head, he saw several horsemen a hundred yards below him. They were Indians.

Mescaleros.

A fierce shout rang out as Fargo sprang to the stallion and vaulted into the saddle. Cutting to the right, he took the opposite slope at breakneck speed. Even with his guns he would be wise to avoid tangling with the war party. For one thing, he had no idea how many there really were. For another, they might get lucky. His best bet was to outrun them.

Fargo reached the flatland and brought the Ovaro to a gallop. Four savage figures were silhouetted on the ridge. A rifle cracked but the range was too great. Whooping and hollering, the warriors thundered in pursuit.

Lashing the reins and lightly using his spurs, Fargo raced like the wind. The Apache mounts were small, wiry, and fleet of foot. Over short distances they could hold their own against the Ovaro, but they lacked the stallion's stamina. That was Fargo's ace in the hole.

The pinto flowed smoothly over the rugged ground. Fargo reached back and palmed the Colt, which he shoved in his holster. Several shots blasted but none came close.

Soon the flatland was replaced by broken terrain. Fargo plunged into a maze of gullies and ravines. Thorny mesquite was thick and he avoided it, as he also avoided slopes covered with loose gravel. A single misstep would prove fatal.

Bit by bit Fargo increased his lead. Howls of frustration rose on his heels. He saw a wide gap in the mesquite and angled in it. Turning a corner, he confronted a solid wall of prickly thorns. He had to haul sharply on the reins to keep from riding pell-mell into the barrier. As it was, the stallion was nicked in several spots.

Fargo fought down fleeting panic. He had blundered into a pocket of clear ground where there was no other way out, and the Apaches would be on him at any moment. He went to wheel, then paused, his gaze drawn to the right where the mesquite curved, forming a shallow gap.

Riding into the gap, Fargo turned. He was near the opening and could hear the Mescaleros coming on strong. They were so intent on overtaking him that they swept around the bend at a reckless speed. Much too late, they saw the wall of mesquite. The foremost warrior tried to rein up but his horse plowed into the barrier. Both man and mount crashed down, thrashing and shrieking. The second Apache fared little better. He hauled on his reins and his animal dug in its hooves and slid to a lurching stop, but as it did, the horse bent its head low and the Apache sailed over its neck into the thorns.

The last two Mescaleros had enough forewarning to come to a stop. It was then, before they collected their wits, that Fargo shot from the gap, streaking between the pair. He clubbed the one on the right across the face even as he drove his left boot into the other one.

In a heartbeat Fargo was out of the pocket and racing to the end of the mesquite patch where he veered to the north. For over a mile he goaded the stallion onward. Repeated glances showed no sign of the Apaches so he slowed to a walk. He had done it. The Mescaleros would be too busy tending to their wounds to come after him.

Only one problem had been solved, though. Uppermost on Fargo's mind was finding the Navaho and Jennifer. To do that, he had to backtrack his own trail. It would be time consuming; he would be fortunate if he overtook them by nightfall.

After permitting the Ovaro to rest, Fargo traveled westward. Noon found him on the ridge where he had revived. By two o'clock he came to the clearing in which they had camped. Dismounting, he studied the tracks.

Coyote had not dawdled. He had saddled the mare, forced Jennifer to ride double, and headed to the south, toward the distant Bar R, just as he had claimed he would do.

Fargo could have gained ground quickly since the mare was so heavily burdened if his own horse were not so tired. He was forced to hold the Ovaro to a brisk walk and had to stop often to give it a breather. The afternoon waxed, then waned. The sun hovered on the horizon when he skirted a hill and beheld a small flock of buzzards wheeling on the air currents a quarter of a mile beyond.

Fearing Jennifer Ragsdale had become the latest victim of the renegades, Fargo made for the spot. A few of the vultures had descended to treetop level but they banked high into the sky as he came near, the flapping of their large wings loud in the silence.

They were circling over a field flanked by short pines. Fargo rose in the stirrups but saw no reason for their interest. The field was empty. He was almost to the middle before he heard a wavering groan and spotted a grisly figure over at the trees.

It was Coyote. Someone had tied his arms and legs to a couple of trees spaced close together, stripped him of clothes and moccasins, and used him for whittling practice. Both his ears were gone, as was most of his nose. A wide patch of skin on his chest had been peeled off, as if someone had begun to skin him alive. His toes were missing. And both eyes had been gouged out.

Fargo drew rein and slid off. His stomach churned and he swallowed bitter bile.

The old man had ceased groaning. He cocked his head and spoke in his own tongue, then a few words in Spanish, and last of all in English, "Who is it? Who is there?"

"Skye Fargo."

Coyote, incredibly, smiled wanly. "You got loose so soon? The last man I tied like that was on his horse for three days." His smile vanished. "I am sorry, white-eye. I could not stop them from taking the pretty one."

"Was it the Apaches or your grandson's gang?"

The warrior tried to answer but was too weak. Fargo walked up to him, wishing he had a canteen or water skin. "Take your time."

Inhaling, Coyote revealed, "The *bandidos* took her. They were on us before I could get away. I told them I was taking her to her family but they would not listen. They accused me of betraying them. They dragged me off the horse and did this." He faltered.

"Don't talk anymore," Fargo said, drawing the toothpick. "I'll cut you down."

"No," Coyote said. "There is only one thing you can do for me." Pausing, he squared his narrow shoulders. "Finish it."

"I wish there was something else I could do," Fargo said in regret. He had misjudged the venerable warrior and wanted to do something to ease the Navaho's suffering, but he couldn't bring himself to slit the man's throat.

"There are other ways," Coyote said weakly. "But first, heed my words. There is something I must tell you, something important." He made a rasping voice and coughed violently. "My . . . my grandson . . ." he began, then stiffened and raised his face to the sky. "I come to you, Earth Mother. My time is done."

Just like that, the warrior died.

Even though every minute counted, Fargo cut Coyote down and buried the warrior in a shallow grave. He placed rocks on the dirt mound to discourage scavengers, found the tracks of a dozen shod horses leading to the southeast, and headed after them.

To the west, the sun sank behind the mountains.

12

Skye Fargo had seldom been so impatient for the sun to rise. He had made another cold camp after pushing on the night before for as long as the lingering light lasted. Once total darkness set in, he'd had no recourse but to stop and await the new day. It had been a long, restless night.

Now, stepping into the stirrups, Fargo tried not to think of what the bandits might have done to Jennifer Ragsdale. Her only hope lay in the fact that women were rare on the frontier, pretty ones even more so. Rather than butcher her as they had Coyote, the cutthroats might want to keep her around awhile. They'd pass her from man to man, taking turns until her body was all used up and she was an emotional wreck. Then they would finish her off with a bullet to the brain. Or maybe they would carve her up some.

Fargo wanted to keep that from happening. The tracks were still plain to see, so before the sun crested the horizon he was bearing due south as the gang had done. Why the gang should go in that direction, he didn't know.

The bandits had made no attempt to hide their trail. Before too long it became apparent that two riders had made a habit of riding a score of feet to one side of the main bunch. Fargo could tell that one of the horses was Jennifer's mare. The other, he figured, must be the bandit picked to guard her. A second possibility was that the renegades had a new leader who was not letting her out of his sight.

Before noon Fargo came on the remains of the camp they had made the night before. He poked a stick in the charred embers of their fire and found some at the bottom which were still warm. The grass had been so trampled by boots and hooves that it was impossible to determine very much.

At sunrise the gang had resumed their journey at a trot. Fargo would have to hurry if he wanted to catch up to them before nightfall. He allowed the Ovaro to rest for only ten minutes, then off he went.

The day turned out to be a scorcher, fit only for lizards and grasshoppers. Objects tended to shimmer in the distance. Twice Fargo thought he saw riders ahead but they turned out to be trees. He had to slow the Ovaro to a walk before too long so the pinto would last the day.

Toward the middle of the afternoon the trail bore to the southeast, into the San Mateo Mountains. Fargo was glad when forest closed around him since it would screen him from prying eyes higher up. He came to a talus slope the bandits had scaled but he went around, knowing from experience that the peal of horseshoes on stone could carry for quite a ways.

It was late afternoon when Fargo paused on a switchback winding down from a divide and spied smoke in a small valley bisected by a stream. At last something had gone in his favor. The gang had made an early camp.

Descending with the utmost caution, Fargo hid the stallion in brush. Bent at the waist, he moved close enough to the smoke to see the oval clearing in which the bandits rested. A burly breed was roasting a fawn over the fire. Another was tending to the horses. At first Fargo saw no sign of Jennifer and worried that they had already disposed of her. Then he spotted the dejected blonde walking along the shallow stream with someone else. His eyes widened in surprise.

Santiago Maxwell was still alive. He wore no hat, and a wide makeshift bandage covered most of his head. His face was much paler than it had been. He moved slowly, undoubtedly still weak from the severe wound.

Automatically Fargo took a steady bead on the killer's head. He was going to finish the job right this time and put a permanent end to the scourge of New Mexico. But as his finger started to close on the trigger, he checked the urge. He had to keep Jennifer's safety in mind above all else. Should Maxwell go down, the others would cut loose wildly and she might be harmed.

Biding his time was the only answer. Fargo lowered the Sharps and crept near enough to overhear conversations. There were eleven bandits, counting their leader. Yet there should be twelve.

The renegades were resting from the long ride. A few were cleaning guns. Others honed blades. A card game was under way in which five of them were taking part.

Jennifer and Maxwell walked to the fire. He poured coffee for her but she shook her head, refusing to take the cup.

"You have to eat and drink sometime," Santiago declared. "I will not let you starve yourself to death."

"Why not?" Jennifer said forlornly. "You're fixing to kill me anyway."

The butcher smirked. "True. But it is I who will decide when and how you die. You have caused me much pain, you and that gringo killer. I want you to suffer the torments of hell before you breathe your last."

Jennifer showed no fear. "Just like you made Coyote suffer? You're a monster, Santiago, a vile, pathetic monster. That kind man was your own grandfather, yet you carved him up and laughed at his misery. I'll never forget his horrible screams."

"He was given his due for turning against me," Maxwell snapped. "He should have brought you back to us, not taken pity on you and tried to get you to your father." Maxwell swallowed some of the coffee intended for her. "Once, my grandfather was a famous warrior. He slew many enemies on raids against the Apaches, the Comanches, and the Mexicans. But he grew soft and weak in his old age. He wanted nothing more to do with killing, and he was always after me to go south of the border and start my life over. The idiot!"

"You could, you know."

"Never!" Maxwell exclaimed. "I have vowed to wage war against the whites until there are none left in the territory, or I am dead. Whichever happens first."

"Do you really think my pa will fall into your trap?"

"You are his daughter, are you not? He will do anything to save you."

Fargo wondered what they were talking about. He wanted to learn more details but Jennifer lapsed into silence and Maxwell lay down to rest. It was to be a short one. Fargo's keen ears had picked up the drum of driving hooves to the northeast. A pair of riders wearing sombreros were bearing down the valley. One of them Fargo recognized.

The bandits looked and saw who it was but they didn't act very surprised and went on about their business. Maxwell sat up, then frowned. "What is he doing here? This I do not need," he said to no one in particular.

Into the clearing rode Diego Rivera and a vaquero. The firebrand wore a mask of outrage which he vented while springing from his sorrel. "What the hell are you doing here, Santiago? And what is *she* doing here?"

Maxwell pointed at the coffeepot. "Hello to you, too, my friend. You are flustered, I can tell. Sit. Relax. We will talk about this like gentlemen."

Diego braced his hands on his hips. "I want answers. When I agreed that you and your men could hide out on our *rancho* whenever you wanted, I did not mean for you to make camp so close to our hacienda. Thank God Pancho saw your smoke before anyone else did."

"Calm yourself," Maxwell urged.

"How can I? Have you lost your senses? What if my father were to find out? You know how he feels about you."

"It would not be healthy for him to try anything," Maxwell said. "Besides, we will only be here until morning. What can one night hurt, *amigo*?"

As usual, the hothead wasn't content to leave well enough alone. Diego snorted in contempt, saying, "I am not your friend, butcher, and I never will be. I only agreed to our arrangement because you are doing that which I long to do, but which my father would never stand for." His features shone with raw hatred. "I want to grind every gringo under my boot heel."

Fargo noticed that Maxwell wasn't offended by the younger

133

Rivera's tone. Or if Maxwell was, he hid it well. Perhaps because the butcher needed to go on using the Rivera ranch as a sanctuary.

"We have a mutual dream," Maxwell said smoothly. "So do not spoil it by being rash. I will post a man to watch the hacienda, and if anyone but you rides toward us, we will be long gone before they get here."

Rivera gestured at Jennifer. "What about her? Her father has been looking for an excuse to attack our ranch and drive us off for years. If he knew she was here, it would be all he needed."

"Calm yourself," the bandit leader stressed. "Right about now one of my men is telling her precious *padre* that we have her. But Ragsdale has no idea where we are. Your ranch is safe."

The news was alarming. Fargo suspected that Maxwell schemed to use Jennifer as bait to lure her father into a trap. But knowing Ragsdale, Fargo could predict that the outcome would not be to Maxwell's liking. If the Riveras should get involved, then the whole region might explode in a frenzy of wanton killing as hatreds long held in check were given free rein. Maybe that was what Maxwell wanted. Maybe the man was far more devious than Fargo gave him credit for being. It was a chilling thought.

"Very well," Diego was saying. "You may stay the night. But keep the fire low and watch the smoke." He mounted, lashed the sorrel, and headed back the way he had come.

The pair were hardly out of the camp when Maxwell declared loud enough for all his men to hear, "One of these days that jackass is in for a big surprise. I will rip his tongue from his mouth and make him eat it."

Chuckles and laughter greeted the remark. Santiago sent one of the cutthroats to the top of a nearby hill. About then, the meat was roasted to a golden brown and the bandits gathered like starving wolves to eat. Lacking utensils, they carved off great chunks with their knives, then sat and ate with much grunting and belching and smacking of lips.

The scene reminded Fargo of feeding time at a pig farm. Jennifer once again refused to eat, even after Maxwell cuffed her. Bleeding from both lips, she sank onto her side and curled into a ball. Maxwell kicked her but she refused to stir.

Meanwhile, Fargo had made up his mind what he should do. First, he would get her out of there. Second, he would race to the Bar R and warn Ragsdale. By foiling Santiago's plot, he would nip the bloodshed in the bud, sparing the lives of many innocent people.

The sun seemed to take forever to set. The aroma of the roast meat made Fargo's stomach growl so loud he was afraid one of the bandits would hear it. The gang finished off the fawn down to the last morsel. One man went so far as to crack open the bigger bones with a rock and suck the marrow out.

After the meal a bottle of whiskey was passed around. Each man was permitted a few sips, that was all. Cards were produced and a game of stud poker was soon under way. Other bandits rolled dice.

Fargo saw Maxwell try to get Jennifer to talk. When she refused, he kicked her a few times, then joined the card game. The only *bandido* moving around was a lean bandit who verified the horses were tethered and took a seat to watch the players. Gradually twilight shrouded the terrain. Dancing firelight was reflected by the hard faces ringing the flames.

Holding the Sharps close to his left side, Fargo crawled toward the stream. The mounts were tied close to it. He paused now and again to insure he had not drawn the interest of any of the cutthroats. It helped that his buckskins were the same color as the brush and his face was streaked with dust.

The horses were munching grass, except for two or three which stood with tired head hung low. Fargo was almost abreast of the line when a gelding gazed in his general direction. The wind was blowing from the string to him so he knew the animals hadn't caught his scent. He froze until the gelding looked away.

At last Fargo gained the low bank. Sliding through dry weeds, he slid down to the water and set the Sharps on a dry patch of gravel. Then, on his hands and knees, he moved parallel with the stream until he was near the first horse. It was too busy grazing to pay much attention to him. Palming the Arkansas toothpick, he inched high enough to cut the tether.

Down the line Fargo went, freeing every animal. He relied on the horses being either too hungry or too tired to stray off and not one disappointed him. When the last mount had been tended to, Fargo silently worked his way to a point due north of Jennifer Ragsdale. She was closest to the water but her back was to him.

Groping the ground, Fargo found several pebbles. Careful not to raise his head too high, he threw one of them at the woman's back and flattened in case any of the bandits should glance up. When he dared to peek, Jennifer had not budged. He figured that he had missed and tried the next pebble, but this time he kept his eyes above the bank level so he could see how she reacted.

The small stone hit Jennifer in the small of the back. She reached behind her and swatted the air a few times as if trying to smash a mosquito.

Fargo used the third pebble, aiming for the back of her head. She started when it hit her, shifted, and peered into the night. Since there was no other means of letting her know it was him, Fargo popped up high enough for her to see him, then dropped down before any of the bandits could notice.

Jennifer flared to life. Sitting, she brushed bits of grass from her dress while observing the various gang members. "Excuse me," she said to Maxwell. "I need to go into the bushes."

Santiago was studying his hand. "So, you still live after all. I was beginning to have my doubts." He motioned testily. "Go on. Vega, go along, but give her some privacy. White women are touchy about their bodily functions."

A short bandit watching the game frowned and stood. He put a hand on his pistol but did not draw it.

"Thank you, Max," Jennifer said sweetly. Standing, she walked slowly toward the stream.

Fargo moved into the inky shadow of a tree, the toothpick clutched close to his knee. He focused on the guard, on a spot midway down the man's chest. The half-breed was not very

136

pleased at having to go along and kept glancing at the card-players.

Jennifer walked slowly. At the edge of the water she smiled at Vega and said, "You stay here. I'll go across and be right back."

"No, senorita," the breed said. " I must go with you."

"Didn't you hear Max?" Jennifer held her ground. "He told you I was to have some time to myself." She raised the hem of her dress and waded into the water. "Be a decent human being for a change. I won't be long."

The bluster worked. Vega stayed where he was.

Fargo was in motion before she reached the other side. From where Vega stood, only a few of the bandits could see him and none were looking in his direction. Fargo swooped out of the shadows to clamp a forearm across the man's windpipe. He buried the toothpick to the hilt between two of the killer's ribs. It all happened so swiftly that the stunned Vega did no more than gasp and sputter and then go limp, dead on his feet, his heart pierced.

Fargo quickly lowered the body and hauled the man close to the tree. A glance at the camp confirmed none of the bandits had heard. A tall renegade had just told a joke and many were laughing.

For once Jennifer knew just what to do. She hurried across the stream and gently gripped his elbow. "Just when I had given up all hope, you came back for me," she whispered. "I'm yours forever."

Fargo didn't like the sound of that but it was the wrong time and place to point out she was taking an awful lot for granted. "No chatter," he said gruffly while steering her to the west. They crept past the horses, a few of which had strayed a yard or two but not far enough to be obvious to the bandits.

Retrieving the Sharps, Fargo gestured for Jennifer not to move. Then, gliding up the bank close to the string, he cocked the rifle. A few of the horses looked at him. Beyond them the bandits idled away the evening. He saw Maxwell glance toward the stream.

"Vega? What is keeping that woman so long?"

Fargo sighted on the butcher's chest but once again fate intervened and a horse blocked the shot. To wait any longer invited discovery. Fargo let out with an bloodcurdling Apache war whoop even as he pointed the rifle at the ground and squeezed the trigger. The effect on the horses was electrifying. Whirling, they bolted, straight at the bewildered bandits.

Curses and screams rang out as Fargo dashed to Jennifer, grabbed her warm hand, and sped into the brush. He saw the bandits scrambling out of the path of their panicked mounts. One man was too slow and went down under flailing hooves. His screams only spurred the horses to greater speed.

It had worked like a charm. Fargo reached the stallion without mishap and helped Jennifer up before climbing on himself. They had to ride so close together that her hair was inches below his nose and his manhood rubbed against her backside. He headed south, trying not to dwell on the friction warming his loins.

When they had gone over a mile and the bandits had not yet appeared, Fargo felt it safe to slow to a walk. The Ovaro was tired. He had to conserve its energy, and his own, for when it was most needed.

"Can I talk now?" Jennifer asked softly, turning. Her mouth ended up so close to his that her breath fanned his lips.

"All you want to," Fargo said, steeling himself against her charms. "By morning you'll be home. And if I were you, I'd give serious thought to going to Virginia to stay with your uncle. You'll find a new man in no time."

Her smile was a harbinger of things to come. "I've already found the man of my dreams. You."

Fargo had expected as much. "I'm not ready to settle down and raise a slew of kids. I made that plain to you before. Once I drop you off, I'm out of your life for good."

"I know what you told me, but you can't still mean it. Not after what we did. You've proven that you care by coming back for me."

Why was it, Fargo reflected, that some women would never take a man at his word? He could talk himself blue in the face and they'd still believe what they wanted. It was as if everything he had said had gone in one ear and out the other. Which he should have foreseen. After all, he'd seen how she behaved with Santiago Maxwell. She had shown that when it came to affairs of the heart, she was as blind as a bat.

"You can't deny the truth," Jennifer filled the silence. "I know it's hard for a man to admit that he cares. But I can afford to be patient. Once you open up to me, we'll be together forever."

Trying one last time to spare her feelings, Fargo said, "We all see things differently, Jenny. It pays to remember that just because you think a certain way doesn't mean everyone else will. Look at the two of us. You claim that I love you. I know that I don't. It would be best for both of us if you would see things the way they are and not how you imagine them to be."

For the longest while Jennifer was quiet and Fargo began to think he had made his point. He should have known better.

"Wait until Pa hears. He'll be fit to be tied. But he won't break us up like he did Max and me. If he tries, I'll go off with you and never see him again as long as I live."

Fargo had done his best. "We're not going anywhere together," he declared bluntly. "I don't love you. I can't say it any plainer than that. I'm sorry." She attempted to speak and he cut her off. "I'd be proud to call you a friend, but that's as far as it goes."

"We kissed. We touched. We . . . "

"People kiss and touch all the time but that doesn't mean they are in love. If that's how you see life, then you shouldn't kiss another man until you find one willing to slip a ring on your finger." Fargo was on a roll so he kept on. "And since you brought this up, you might as well know that I doubt Santiago ever truly loved you. No man can care for a woman and beat her like he beat you, no matter what had happened to him."

That shut her up for over two hours. A sliver of moon hung in the sky when next she spoke, her voice low and timid as that of a little girl's would be. "I reckon I've been making a grand fool of myself. I'm not an old hand at handling men, like Virginia is. She's gone through more than I could count."

Fargo saw no need to bring up that he was one of them.

"Santiago was the first guy I ever let touch me, Skye. He was so kind, always flattering me, making me feel special. I assumed it was because he loved me so I gave myself to him. Maybe, though—"Jennifer paused—"maybe you're right. It upsets me to doubt him, but maybe he said all those nice things just so I would give in. Does that ever happen?"

"Men, and women, do it all the time."

"Really? Mercy me. What kind of world am I living in?"

There was no answer to that one. Fargo kept his eyes peeled for a spot to stop for the night. They were in low foothills bordering the plain and he could see the grassland below. For quite some time he had been following a game trail which he hoped would bring them to water. Ahead reared scattered stands of trees. He passed the first cluster.

Suddenly the stallion swung its head to the right.

Before Fargo could do the same, he heard a metallic rasp and a steely warning.

"Stop where you are, gringo. And raise your arms or I will blow your brains out."

13

Skye Fargo had to do what he was told. With the reins in one hand and his other arm looped around Jennifer Ragsdale's slim waist, it would take precious seconds for him to unlimber his Colt, giving the man behind them plenty of time to do as he had threatened. Resigned to obeying, Fargo drew rein. But as he did he contrived to turn the Ovaro to the right so he could see the lanky figure in a sombrero who sat astride a bay near the trees.

Jennifer put a hand to her mouth, then blurted, "I know him! His name is Benito. He's one of Max's men."

"*Sí senorita*," the bandit said. "That I am." Moving the bay closer, he raised his rifle a few inches while glaring at Fargo. "Those arms, gringo. They are not high enough to suit me."

Elevating them, Fargo scanned the stand but saw no sign of any others. For the life of him he couldn't see how Benito's horse had outdistanced the pinto. Then he had a good look at the bay, which glistened dully with sweat, and understood.

"I can't believe you caught us," Jennifer was saying. "How did you trail us in the dark?"

Benito relaxed a little and pushed back his sombrero. "I have not been following you, senorita. I am on my way back from your *rancho*. Santiago sent me to deliver a message to your father." The killer snickered. "That *padre* of yours was mad enough to eat rocks when I left him. It upset him to hear that his little girl had gone and gotten herself captured by his enemies."

The blonde put her hands on the saddle horn as if about to jump down and fly at the bandit. Fargo nudged her with a leg so she would stay where she was. Then he said, "What was the message you relayed?"

"Why should I tell you, gringo bastard? There is no reason you should know."

Jennifer jabbed a finger at the bandit. "I have a good reason, though. Tell me."

Benito balked. "I don't know, senorita. Santiago did not say for me to let you know."

"Did he order you not to tell me?"

"Well, no," Benito admitted. "Very well. I do not see where it can hurt. Santiago told your father that if he wants to see you alive again, he must come alone to Diablo Canyon when the sun is straight overhead tomorrow. If your father does not come, Santiago is going to chop off your head and leave it on the doorstep of your house."

"My pa would never be so stupid as to walk into a trap like that," Jennifer declared. "Especially not on my account."

"I do not know what you mean by that," Benito said, "but you are wrong. Your *padre* said he would show up all by himself and unarmed, just as Santiago wants." The man laughed dryly. "Your father is not very wise. He will never leave the canyon in one piece."

"Pa is willing to sacrifice himself on my account?" Jennifer said in astonishment. "But I didn't think he much cared for me anymore."

Benito came closer still, the rifle trained on Fargo's head. Bending, he snatched the Colt and crammed it under his wide leather belt. He had to tug hard to loosen the Sharps from the boot and placed the big rifle across his thighs. Backing up, he showed his teeth. "There. I have plucked the scorpion's stingers. Now we can all head north. I am sure Santiago will be very glad to see the two of you."

Fargo lifted the reins but Jennifer rested a hand on his wrist, stopping him.

"Wait, Benito," she said. "How would you like five thousand dollars? Or maybe more? If you'll agree to let us go and come with us to the Bar R, I'll see to it that my pa pays you handsomely. You have my word."

The bandit cackled. "What do you take me for? *Estupido?* If I were to show my face on your ranch again, your father would have me strung from a tree." He shook his head. "No, I am too fond of life to run the risk. We will ride north, *por favor.* Santiago wants me to report to him by sunrise, and he does not like it when someone fails to do as he wants. You will go first, of course."

Fargo rode on by. He still had the toothpick nestled inside his right boot. All it would take was for the bandit to get a little too close. But every time he glanced back on the sly, Benito was well out of reach.

Suddenly Fargo became aware that he might not get the chance. The distant rumble of hooves told him that the bandits had recovered their mounts and were out searching for them. In a matter of minutes he would be a prisoner.

Benito also heard, and chuckled. "Unless I miss my guess, gringo, those riders I hear are Santiago and my *compadres.* I hope for your sake that he is in a good mood. If not, I will have to listen to your screams as he peels the skin from your body. It is one of his favorite tortures."

Fargo had a suitable oath on the tip of his tongue when to his dismay Jennifer swung her left leg over to the right side of the stallion, leaped down, and bolted into high weeds.

"What the hell!" he hollered, afraid the killer would plug her in the back. "Get back here!"

"I won't go through that nightmare again! They're not taking me alive!" Jennifer yelled.

Cursing a blue streak, Benito angled the bay toward her and brought up his rifle. "Stop, senorita!" he bellowed. "Stop or I will shoot."

The bandit had made a mistake. He had taken his eyes off Fargo. The bay was only a few feet away, its rump nearly touching the Ovaro's. In a flash Fargo streaked out the throwing knife, twisted, and pushed off with both hands. Benito must have heard the saddle creak because he spun and extended the rifle. Fargo batted it with his left hand while at the same time he alighted on the bay and drove the keen blade into the bandit's jugular. The rifle went off, harmlessly discharging into the ground. Fargo wrenched the toothpick out and struck again, this time sinking the blade into Benito's chest. Gurgling loudly, the bandit let go of the gun to clutch his spurting neck. Fargo grasped his Colt, then shoved Benito off the bay.

Jennifer had stopped. "You did it!" she exclaimed, happily clapping. "I knew you could!"

It dawned on Fargo that she had made the break on purpose to afford him the chance to dispose of Benito. Looking down, he saw the bandit trying to draw a pistol with a hand so slick with blood that Benito couldn't get a firm grip. Fargo had no such problem. He planted two slugs in Benito's chest. When the killer slumped, Fargo jumped off and cast about for the Sharps, which had fallen during their struggle. He located it and stepped to the Ovaro as the blonde sprinted up.

"It's a crying shame you're not the marrying kind," she said. "A woman never needs to fret for her life with a man like you around."

It was hardly the time to discuss matrimony again. Fargo pushed her toward the bay. "Get on. We're not out of the woods yet, not by a long shot."

Once they were both on horseback, Fargo turned due east. Jennifer was none too pleased and called out, "Shouldn't we be heading south, toward the Bar R?"

"Use your noggin. That's the way they'll expect us to go." Fargo bent low and she was bright enough to follow his example. They had to cover over a hundred yards before they came to scrub trees, where they halted so Fargo could survey the crest of the hill. It wasn't long before a large cluster of dark riders thundered to the spot where Benito had fallen.

Santiago's roar of rage was like that of a wounded grizzly. There was a brief flurry of words too faint to make out, then the entire band rumbled to the south.

Jennifer giggled as might a child playing hide-and-seek. "Look at those dunderheads! You'd think they'd give up. They're never going to catch us."

Fargo thought of the two bandits who had died at the camp, and Benito. "Maxwell won't rest until he does to us what he did to Coyote. In his eyes we have a lot to answer for."

"As if he doesn't," Jennifer said. "Once, I would have defended him with my dying breath. Now I can't wait for him to pay for his terrible crimes." She paused. "Oh, my God! I almost forgot! What about my pa?"

"We have to stop him before he rides into Maxwell's trap," Fargo agreed. He scratched his chin, trying to recollect exactly where Diablo Canyon was located. While he had been through the region before, he didn't know every landmark. Diablo Canyon failed to ring a bell. Then he remembered that *diablo* was Spanish for devil, and there was a rugged, remote canyon by that name to the southwest. "Our best bet is to reach Devil Canyon before your father does. If I'm right, it's about a ten-hour ride west of here so we'd better start right away."

"What if we don't make it in time?" Jennifer responded. "No, I say we head straight for the Bar R."

"And if we get there after he's left? Or run into the bandits?" Fargo shook his head. "It's not what I'd do. But he's your father so I'll go along with whatever you want."

Jennifer bit her lip and stared first to the south and then the southwest. "Dear Lord. His life is in my hands. I can't let him down." Torn by indecision, she folded her hands and gazed at the stars. "What do I do? I can't make up my mind."

Fargo sat quietly. It had to be her decision. Small wonder it was so hard for her, since her father had been telling her what to do and when to do it for so many years, she seldom had to decide things for herself. Her sheltered life hadn't prepared her for dealing with the real world, as she had proved in her choice of suitors.

"I think you're right," Jennifer said. "My pa will probably get an early start, long before we could reach the Bar R. And with the bandits now between us and the ranch, it's better to head for Devil's Canyon."

So they did. But it soon was apparent to Fargo that they would be hard-pressed to get there before noon. The Ovaro and the bay had been ridden hard for many miles. Both needed rest, and lots of it. Yet if they stopped, William Ragsdale was as good as dead. He compromised and held the horses to a walk for the first few hours.

The slow pace aggravated Jennifer. She complained bitterly several times, urging him to gallop. His refusal made her mad and she sulked until daylight, not saying a word.

Devil Canyon was situated in an arid spine of stark mountains. No one ever went there, unless it was Apaches or outlaws. As canyons went, it was not very big. A mile and a half from end to end and perhaps a quarter of a mile wide, there was no water and no vegetation of any kind.

Fargo yawned often. He needed rest just as much, if not more, than the stallion, but he had to stay awake to see the ordeal through.

Sunrise made traveling easier. They could see obstacles clearly and also spot objects far off. Fargo caught sight of antelope and deer and once saw a female bear and a cub on a knoll.

Jennifer, who had fallen behind when she started pouting, rode up alongside the pinto. "Do you reckon we'll make it there before Pa does?"

"Time will tell," was all Fargo could say. It would be nip and tuck, but he had high hopes they would reach the canyon well before midday.

"I've never been through the Black Range before," Jennifer said nervously. "Pa told all the hands to fight shy of it. He said it's crawling with Apaches."

She was right, but Fargo saw no need to add to her worries. The Black Range, favorite haunt of the Mescaleros, flanked the Continental Divide. Once over a pass he remembered, they would be close to the canyon. The hard part was the long, arduous climb to get there. It was a trek that would tire bighorn sheep.

By the middle of the morning, with the warm sun on their backs, they came to a shelf. Fargo stopped. "We'll rest here a few minutes, then push on."

"But I'm not very tired."

Fargo eased from the saddle. "I was thinking of the horses, not us. It's hell from here on up." Dropping the reins, he stepped to the edge. From their vantage point they had a panoramic view of the countryside. He could see for miles. It bothered him that nowhere to the east was there sign of a dust plume. As if Jennifer could read his mind, she commented on the same thing.

"Shouldn't we be able to spot Max's bunch from up here?"

"You'd think so."

"Does that mean we're so far ahead of them that we can breathe easy for a spell?" She pursed those rosy lips of hers. "Or does it mean we're so far behind them that we'll be too late?"

Fargo took off his hat to run a hand through his hair. "You keep asking questions no one can answer. We'll have to wait and see."

Jennifer touched his arm. "I want you to know that whatever happens, I'll always be in your debt. Maybe we can't be husband and wife. And maybe we can't even be lovers anymore. But I'll never forget you, Skye Fargo, not as long as I draw breath."

Adjusting his hat, Fargo walked to the stallion to check the cinch. He refrained from telling Jennifer that if it weren't for her, he would have gone on to Las Cruces long ago and left William Ragsdale to reap the harvest of hatred he had sown. His true sympathies were with Hernando Rivera, not Ragsdale.

"Skye! Look!"

Turning, Fargo saw her pointing up the mountain. Tendrils of dust far above them marked the passage of a large group of horsemen.

"The bandits, you figure?"

Although Fargo had intended to rest longer, the pathetic expression she wore goaded him into forking leather yet again. He had to slap his boots against the pinto's hide to prod the stallion into motion. The Ovaro was reluctant to make the climb and Fargo couldn't blame it. Not only were the slopes much too steep, countless boulders had to be skirted and talus slopes had to be negotiated with the utmost care.

It was the middle of the morning before a rocky notch appeared. "The pass," Fargo said for Jennifer's benefit. "Another hour and we'll be there."

"What happened to the riders we spotted? There hasn't been a trace of them."

Actually, there had been. Earlier on Fargo had come on the tracks of nine or ten horses and swung wide of them to spare her more anxiety. It had to be the bandits, he figured. Maxwell would reach Devil Canyon long before they did.

The notch was much as Fargo remembered it from the last time he had been there, almost four years ago. A number of jagged sections of cliff wall had given way and partially blocked the opening but there was still enough room for a horse to pass. He placed a hand on the Colt just in case Maxwell had left someone to keep an eye out for Ragsdale.

Here in the narrow defile the wind shrieked and howled like a pack of ravening wolves. It cooled Fargo's face. He barely noticed, so intent was he on the towering ramparts, which seemed to brush the sky. Here and there boulders were precariously balanced, and he could imagine one of them crashing down with hardly a nudge. The blast of a gunshot might be more than enough.

Jennifer was also scanning the heights, so she never saw the many tracks plain as day in the dust underfoot. Fargo did, and it did not bode well.

Presently they emerged onto a winding bench which wound toward Devil Canyon three miles distant. The earth had been chewed up by heavy hooves. Fargo couldn't be positive because individual prints were hard to identify, but it seemed as if Santiago Maxwell had more men with him than he had the night before. Finally, Jennifer noticed.

"We're too late, Skye! I've let my pa down. He'll be killed because of me." She was as pale as paper. "I'll never be able to live with myself."

Fargo moved to a gentle slope and went over the lip. "There you go again, jumping to conclusions. Give your father more credit. He hasn't lasted this long by being soft." It rankled him to compliment the man who had caused all the bloodshed but he needed her to stay calm.

"True enough. Ma likes to say that Pa is as hard as iron and as prickly as a cactus. If anyone can turn the tables on Max, he can."

The country here was much drier, the trees fewer and far between, the ground parched for water which fell all too rarely. Fargo stuck to the trail left by the renegades since they knew the shortest route to the canyon and how to enter it once there. He was not worried about overtaking them. The bandits were a good thirty minutes ahead, a fact he did not mention to Jennifer Ragsdale.

The sun arched higher. It was almost directly above them when Fargo reined up in a dry wash a stone's throw from the mouth of Devil Canyon, which wound off to the north. Maxwell had not missed a trick. The bandits had stuck to the thickest cover and used washes and gullies to keep out of sight.

Jennifer bobbed her head at the clear stretch between the wash and the canyon. "What are we waiting for? Every second counts."

"It wouldn't do to give ourselves away," Fargo said. "If I was Maxwell, I'd have a man watching to signal when your father shows up. We should swing wide and look for another way in."

"We don't have the time!"

Fargo looked at her. "If we're killed, who helps your father then?" She had no retort so he went back up the wash to a point where part of the slope had buckled. He trotted up this natural ramp and through chaparral to a bluff which overlooked Devil Canyon. Dismounting, he hid the horses, laid hold of the Sharps, and went the rest of the way on foot, striding quickly. Jennifer did her best to keep up, taking two steps for every one of his.

The crown of the bluff was flat and covered with low brush. Fargo worked along until he came to a shallow bowl which formed part of the west rim. From there he could see a good portion of Devil Canyon, including the opening. He also sped a way down into it. "How are you at climbing?" he asked.

Jennifer leaned out to see better. "I wasn't a tomboy like my sister when I was younger, but I think I can manage."

"Let's find out."

All went well until they were close to the bottom. They clambered over outcroppings, shimmied down a cleft, and picked their way along a ledge no wider than their feet. Then they were confronted by a sheer rock wall over nine feet high.

"I'll go first," Fargo said, bunching his leg muscles. He jumped, the Sharps held overhead so the stock wouldn't break if he landed poorly. As he came down, he bent his knees. The jolt still rocked him and he nearly pitched onto his side. Keeping his balance, he leaned the rifle against the wall, then beckoned.

Jennifer appeared uneasy. Licking her lips, she gauged the height, closed her eyes, and flung herself into the air. It was rash and reckless and nearly resulted in disaster.

Fargo saw that she had leaped at the wrong angle and he had to scoot backward so she wouldn't land on top of him. Bracing himself, he held out both arms. Catching her was like catching a falling tree. She nearly slammed him to the ground, but he threw himself forward at the instant she hit his arms, countering some of the impact. As it was, he staggered and would have fallen had he not ignored the pain in his lower back and thighs and dug in his heels.

Opening her eyes, Jennifer saw that she was safe and grinned. "That wasn't so bad after all. I thought I'd break a bone."

Setting her down, Fargo claimed the Sharps. They were now on the canyon floor within forty yards of the opening. Boulders and brush blocked their view of the middle of the canyon, so they advanced stealthily. Or as stealthily as they could with Jennifer constantly trying to get past Fargo so she could take the lead. She forgot all about setting down her feet exactly where he did and displayed her old knack for stepping on every dry twig in her path. Several times he put a finger to his lips but she was too distraught to heed him.

The whole time, Fargo had a gut feeling that unseen eyes were on them. It was so strong that he wanted to stop and lay low until he could be sure it just wasn't a case of raw nerves. But Jennifer was not about to halt short of being shot dead so he hiked on until they reached a boulder the size of the line shack.

Fargo stepped to the right and stared out across Devil Canyon. When he spotted a lone figure standing sixty feet away, he flattened against the boulder and brought the Sharps up.

"Don't shoot!" Jennifer exclaimed. "That's my pa!"

So it was. William Ragsdale stood there in the glaring sunlight as calmly as if he were in church, his arms folded across his broad chest, a Colt high on his right hip, a cigar jutting from his mouth. His gaze was fixed on the mouth of the canyon, and he was smirking.

"We have to go to him!" Jennifer said, trying to step around Fargo.

"Not yet. Something isn't right. We should wait."

"Like hell. I have to be at his side when Max gets here. My pa isn't facing those vile butchers alone."

Fargo held her arm to keep her from going anywhere. She pulled back, then raised a hand to slap him. They both heard a gun being cocked to their rear and whirled. Fargo thought it would be one of Santiago Maxwell's men or Maxwell himself. But it wasn't.

Virginia Ragsdale, a gleaming pistol steady in her right hand, grinned at him. "Put down the rifle, lover." When he had, she snickered and said, "So. Should I shoot you now or give my pa the privilege?"

14

Skye Fargo saw relief wash over Jennifer Ragsdale. Disregarding the pistol, she dashed over to her sister and gestured frantically.

"Ginny! Thank heaven you've come! Pa is in great danger. We have to help him."

The redhead sneered. "Don't get your bloomers in an uproar, princess. Pa is fine. You really don't think he'd let breed trash like Maxwell get the better of him, do you?" Virginia indicated the canyon floor. "Cole Barton, Bo Weaver, and sixteen of our best hands are all close by, ready to cut loose when Pa gives the signal. Santiago Maxwell won't know what hit him, I reckon."

Tears of joy rimmed Jennifer's grateful eyes. "Oh, I can't tell you how this makes me feel. I thought Pa was a goner on account of me."

Virginia's sneer widened. "You sure do have a puny thinker, girl. Pa wouldn't throw his life away for the likes of you. The only reason he came is to wipe out the bandits once and for all." She shifted a leg and winced. "We had to ride like hell to get here well before noon. I don't mind telling you I'm sore in places I've never been sore before."

Jennifer blinked, dabbed a hand at the corner of her right eye, and said bleakly, "Pa didn't come here to save me?"

Low laughter greeted the question. "You sure do rate yourself awful high in Pa's affections, Jenny," Virginia said cruelly. "Much higher than he rates you. To tell you the truth, he half figured you might be in cahoots with Maxwell—"

"I'd never!" Jennifer cried out.

"Keep your voice down, damn it. Do you want to give us away? The bandits might be close enough to hear."

Fargo was being ignored, which suited him just fine. On the sly he had slid his right hand close enough to his Colt to risk a draw. He glanced out at William Ragsdale. The rancher must have heard his daughter's cry because he was staring at the boulder, perturbed. Ragsdale took a step toward them but then his head snapped up and he faced the canyon mouth.

Virginia was speaking harshly. "Pa went into a rage when Fargo and you couldn't be found, girl," she revealed. "He figured the two of you had gone and run off together until one of the hands pointed out that the tracks showed you had left first all by your lonesome and that Fargo here had trailed you. So Pa guessed that you were going to see the breed." She poked her sister with the revolver. "He was right, wasn't he? You disgraced yourself even more, didn't you?"

The blood had drained from Jennifer's features. "I've learned my lesson," she said solemnly. "Santiago nearly killed me. If not for Skye, we wouldn't be standing here."

"Skye, is it?" Virginia said, aflame with resentment. "Well, ain't this a hoot. There isn't another man alive who can claim he's had both of us." She looked at him. "So tell me. Which one of us is the best? As if I don't already know."

At that juncture the canyon echoed to the arrival of a large body of horsemen. Virginia, forgetting herself, dashed to the edge of the boulder, next to Fargo. Jennifer merely bowed her head, tears trickling down her cheeks.

Fargo had had enough surprises for one day. He didn't need another. Yet that is exactly what he got when he saw the newcomers. It should have been Santiago Maxwell and the cutthroats. Instead, of all people, it was Hernando Rivera, his son Diego, who looked miserable, and eight heavily armed vaqueros.

William Ragsdale was equally surprised but he recovered quickly and broke out in a sinister smile. "Rivera! As I live and breathe!" he bellowed. "What the hell are you doing here?"

Rivera's party reined up in a cloud of dust. Hernando rose

in the stirrups to scour the canyon but did not glance toward the boulder screening Fargo and the women. "I came to warn you, Senor Ragsdale," he announced loudly. "I hope that by doing this, we can put the past behind us and live in peace from now on."

Ragsdale tilted his head. "Warn me?"

"Do not play games with me. I know why you are here," Hernando said, and gave his son a smack on the arm. "I forced the truth out of Diego after a dead *bandido* was found on my property and one of my vaqueros told me that he had seen Diego talking to Santiago Maxwell." Hernando was sincere when he added, "It pains me to think of your daughter in the clutches of that monster."

"That's damned decent of you," Ragsdale said, and chuckled. "Not that I believe you, you being a greaser and all. I figure you're working with Maxwell, just like I claimed all along."

Rivera stiffened. "If that were so, would I have worn out good horses racing here to help you?"

The beefy rancher shrugged. "Who can say how a Mex's mind works? All I can tell you is that you made a big mistake, mister. You rode right into a trap I set for Maxwell." Ragsdale snapped his fingers and his men popped up, among them the Texas gunman and the foreman, rifles ready to fire. They had been secreted behind boulders on both sides of the canyon. "Seems to me that I can kill two birds with one stone. First you, then that mangy half-breed when he shows his ugly face."

Fargo couldn't stand there idle while Rivera and the vaqueros were wiped out. He started forward but froze when a gun barrel was jammed into his spine.

"No you don't, handsome," Virginia Ragsdale warned. "It's time that greaser got what was coming to him."

Suddenly Jennifer was there, livid with outrage. "But that's not right! Mr. Rivera came here to help. Pa can't kill him."

"You just watch," Virginia declared.

The fate of dozens of lives hung in the balance. Rivera's vaqueros had their hands on their guns but had not yet pulled any hardware, while the Bar R cowboys were awaiting the word from their boss to open fire.

At that precise moment, thundering into Devil Canyon with their six-shooters and rifles blazing, charged Santiago Maxwell and the rest of the bloodthirsty renegades. Yipping like Comanches, they fanned out, shooting at anyone and everyone.

It was easy for Fargo to guess what had happened. Maxwell had been watching the whole time and must have cackled with cold glee when he saw he could get rid of Ragsdale and the Riveras in one fell swoop. It was an opportunity the butcher could not pass up, even if the odds were not in his favor. Or were they? For as Fargo looked on, Bo Weaver shot a vaquero from the saddle and was in turn cored through the head by Diego Rivera.

All hell broke loose. Bandits were firing at cowboys and vaqueros, cowboys and vaqueros were firing at each other and at the bandits. The booming din rocked the canyon walls. Men cursed and screamed. Horses whinnied and plunged in a panic. Dust rose thick into the air, choking animals and men alike. It was a chaotic scene of total slaughter, nightmare carnage made real by a madman's bloodlust.

"Pa!" Virginia called out as dust enveloped him. "He'll be mowed down!" She took two steps, that was all, and stopped short as if she had run into an invisible wall.

Fargo heard the smack of two slugs which struck her high in the chest. He got his arms out and caught her as she fell. Another bullet zinged off the boulder as he lowered her to the dry earth. She gawked at him, in near shock, a pair of red stains spreading rapidly on the front of her outfit.

"Someone shot me?" Virginia said. "They can't do that. I don't want to die." And then she did, her eyelids fluttering like her breath. She quivered a few times and was still.

"No!" Jennifer wailed, falling on her knees beside her sister. "Oh, God. Ginny! Speak to me!" Grabbing the redhead's shoulders, Jennifer shook her. "Please speak to me!"

Several bullets churned up the ground around them. Fargo scooped Jennifer into his left arm and hauled her back behind the boulder despite her efforts to break free. She kicked and clawed and was almost hysterical.

"Let go of me, damn it! She's my sister! I have to help her! She's wounded, not dead."

"Virginia is gone," Fargo declared, setting her down. Jennifer promptly lunged to her feet and dashed toward the prone figure. Again Fargo heard the squishy thud of a slug hitting home. Jennifer Ragsdale spun half around, a hand pressed to her shoulder. In a bound Fargo reached her and helped her sit with her back to the boulder. He went to examine the wound. Suddenly a shadow materialized to his right. Someone was slinking around the boulder toward them.

"Stay put," Fargo whispered, and broke to the left, hugging the rough surface until he came up on a lone renegade who held a pair of smoking pistols. The killer nudged Virginia with a boot, then stepped over her body. Thanks to the bedlam, the man never realized Fargo was there. He extended the Colt and tapped the killer on the shoulder blade. "Looking for someone?"

The renegade whirled but he was far too slow. Fargo stroked the trigger and had the satisfaction of seeing a neat hole blossom in the center of the bandit's forehead. Dead on his feet, the cutthroat swayed. Fargo shoved and the body crashed down, then he darted behind the boulder to tend Jennifer. Only she was gone.

Fargo sprinted to the left again in time to glimpse her stagger into the swirling dust cloud, no doubt going to her father's aid. Cocking the Colt, Fargo plunged in after her. Immediately he was engulfed by clinging dust. He couldn't see more than a few yards in any direction.

On all sides the battle raged. Fargo could make out the shapes of horses and men on foot. Guns spewed flame and lead. Deadly hornets whizzed on by. Fargo crouched low to reduce the odds of being hit by a wild slug. Swinging from side to side, he sought sign of Jennifer Ragsdale.

From somewhere in the midst of the clamor rose a woman's piercing scream.

Fargo made for the sound. He had to jump over the body of a bullet-riddled cowboy. A few feet away lay a dead vaquero. He thought that he spotted Jennifer but when he reached the spot she was gone.

Not having any idea where he was in relation to the boulder or anything else, Fargo moved on, hoping to get clear of the dust. To his left a stricken horse thrashed. Off to the right a man whined that he had been gut shot. Suddenly a gust of wind dispersed some of the cloud and Fargo saw Diego Rivera a dozen feet in front of him. The firebrand saw him at the same moment. While Fargo despised Diego for harboring the bandits, he had no personal quarrel with the man and was content to let him go his way. Diego Rivera, however, snarled, wheeled his mount, and attacked.

Fargo dived to one side as the horse sped toward him. It went by in a flash of hooves, mane, and tail. A bullet kicked up dirt inches from his face. Fargo rolled, pushed to one knee, and aimed. Or wanted to, but there was no one to shoot at. The younger Rivera had disappeared into the roiling cloud.

Going on, Fargo flattened when a volley erupted directly in front of him. By some miracle he was spared. An answering volley kept him low, but when the shooting tapered off, he rose and bolted to the left. For yards on end he hurtled through the blinding pale veil, the dust getting into his nose, his mouth, his throat. He coughed to clear it and someone snapped a shot at the sound which nearly took his head off.

"Pa! Pa!"

The outcry drew Fargo to the right. He swatted at the clinging cloud, but it was like swatting at pea soup. Then he broke into a clear pocket and spied the Texas gunman moving in the same direction. He also saw a pair of mounted renegades beyond Barton, closing in fast. As yet, the gunman had not noticed them. "Barton, to your right!" he shouted.

Texans were known to be handier with six-guns than most everyone else, and the man William Ragsdale had hired was one of the elite. In a blur Cole Barton pivoted and fired from the hip, twin shots banging as one. The head of each bandit snapped backward and both men catapulted over the rumps of their mounts. Barton, instead of being grateful, glared at Fargo. "Damn. Now I'm more obliged to you than ever. Thanks a lot."

The cloud abruptly parted, spewing out of its depths Diego Rivera, who had his revolver leveled and a crazed gleam in his eyes. Diego was almost on top of the Texan. Cole Barton spun. Rivera fired before the gunman could thumb back the hammers, and Barton, jolted, staggered but stayed on his feet. The Texan raised his right arm. Before he could squeeze the trigger Diego's horse rammed into him, knocking him flat. A flying hoof caught Barton on the side of the head, sending his hat flying. Rivera reined up, shifted, and sighted to finish the gunman off.

Fargo was in motion, running toward them. "Diego!" he yelled. "Over here!"

Rivera jerked around. "You!" he hissed.

Their gunshots were a heartbeat apart. Wind fanned Fargo's ear, while his slug penetrated the fleshy part of Diego Rivera's throat and exploded out the side of Rivera's head just below the ear. The hatred on Rivera's face evaporated as the man oozed lifeless from the saddle.

Fargo dashed to the Texan. Barton had been shot above the heart and would have died anyway had Rivera's horse not caved in part of his skull. He had died on his feet, a gun in each hand, and wearing his boots. No Texan could ever ask for more.

A ragged exchange of shots told Fargo the battle was far from over. He resumed his hunt for Jennifer, studying the bodies he came across in case she had fallen too. A riderless horse swept down on him, nearly trampling him in its bid to escape the madness. He grasped at the reins but they slipped through his grip, searing his palm with pain.

Fargo ran on, still not knowing where he was. A boulder loomed before him and he skirted it. Then he heard a sniffle at its base.

Jennifer Ragsdale was on her knees, slumped over, her shoulder soaked from her loss of blood. She was crying silently, the tears a torrent, her whole frame quaking. Glancing up, she tried to speak but couldn't, not until she coughed and swallowed. "He struck me, Skye."

Fargo hunkered and put a hand on her good shoulder. "Who did? Maxwell?"

"No. My own father."

There was no sign of the rancher or anyone else in their

vicinity. Fargo gave her a friendly squeeze and tried to goad her into standing so they could get out of there before one of the renegades spotted them. But she simply knelt there, blubbering like a child who had had its heart crushed.

"I finally found him," Jennifer said in a rush. "I ran up and tried to hug him, to tell him how worried I was, to let him know how much I cared." She squeezed her eyes tight shut. "You should have seen the loathing on his face. He looked at me as if I were the scum of the earth. And do you know what he said?"

"No," Fargo said, keeping close watch on the ring of dust.

"'Get away from me, you little tramp'!" Jennifer doubled over, groaning. "He called me, his daughter, a tramp! Here I thought that deep down, despite all that happened, he still cared for me. At least a little. But Sis was right. He hates me, Skye. He wants nothing to do with me."

"It's his loss," Fargo said. He prided at her arm. "Come on, Jenny. We have to find somewhere you'll be safe."

"No. Leave me." Jennifer pulled her arm loose and leaned against the boulder. "I don't care whether I live or die anymore."

The way Fargo saw it, he had three choices. He could leave her there to be finished off by a renegade or a stray shot. He could drag her with him, which would slow him down and put both of them in greater danger. Or he could slug her and tote her off against her will.

It wasn't hard to make up his mind.

Bending, Fargo draped her unconscious form over his left shoulder. He rose and backpedaled, listening to footsteps rush toward them. Seconds later a bewildered vaquero burst out of the dust. He saw them and began to bring his pistol to bear, then stopped. Fargo recalled having seen the man once before, on the trail from Socorro when he had stopped Barton from throwing down on Hernando.

The vaquero touched his sombrero in salute and turned to run off. A slug smashed into his face, flattening him.

Another whined above Fargo. A shadowy shape lurked in the cloud, shooting at anything that moved. Fargo returned the favor and saw the man pitch over. In the lull that followed, he jogged in the opposite direction. In less than a minute the dust fell behind him and he breathed in fresh air again.

A cluster of boulders offered shelter from the flying lead. As Fargo gently placed Jennifer between two of them, he realized the gunfire had stopped. It was as quiet as a cemetery except for a dull ringing in his ears. Working quickly, he arranged dry brush over Jennifer. When he was convinced no one could find her, he reloaded the Colt and went in search of the two men whose hatred had been the spark which ignited the bloody wildfire of pure slaughter.

The dust was settling rapidly. Bodies were everywhere, bandits and cowboys and vaqueros all mixed together, men who had despised one another sharing the canyon floor as their final resting place. It hadn't mattered to the bullets which struck them low whether they were white or Mexican or halfbreeds. Death made no such distinctions. Dead was dead.

A number of wounded lay among the lifeless. Some groaned in agony. Others called out for help. A few, so weak they could barely move, were trying to stand.

Fargo passed the boulder Jennifer had been behind, then drew up. Hernando Rivera was kneeling, Diego's head cradled in his lap. The father cried without shame. On spying Fargo, he motioned for Skye to come nearer.

"My precious son!" Hernando choked out. "He is gone because I tried to save a man who would have killed me this day if he had the chance. Was I a fool, senor? Where is the justice in that, I ask you?"

It was a question no one could answer and Fargo was not going to try. He left the elder Rivera to his remorse and went on, studying the bodies. Ragsdale and Maxwell were not among them. Where had they gone? Fargo wondered. Pausing, he debated what to do. Nearby lay a Henry repeater. It reminded him of the Sharps, which he had left to the east behind the huge boulder.

The rancher and the renegade would have to wait, Fargo mused. He ran to the boulder and frowned on seeing Virginia's body caked thick with dust. The Sharps was where he had left it. As his fingers curled around the barrel, a mocking laugh pricked the short hairs at the nape of his neck.

"I would not lift that if I were you, gringo," Santiago Maxwell said. "You will live a few moments longer if you do not."

Fargo had the Colt in his right hand, close to his waist. It was possible the butcher had not seen it. Turning just his head, he saw Maxwell covering him with a cocked Spencer. "So you're still alive," he said calmly.

"That I am. Which is more than I can say for my men." Maxwell took a few steps, that mocking grin of his firmly in place. "But then, I can always find many more just like them. In no time I will have a new gang and be peeling off the hides of worthless gringos like yourself."

"I don't think so," Fargo said softly.

"Oh?" Maxwell chortled. "And why is that?"

"Because you're dead."

Fargo ducked and fired in one smooth motion, fanning the Colt since the range was so short, ripping four slugs into Santiago Maxwell as the Spencer boomed and the bullet ricocheted off the boulder. The scourge of New Mexico attempted to work the lever of his rifle but lacked the strength. Wearing a look of utter disbelief, he fell, his face crunching on some rocks.

"I couldn't have done better myself, mister."

Skye Fargo spun to the right where William Ragsdale stood with a Colt in hand. "How long were you there?" he demanded.

"Long enough."

"Why didn't you shoot him?" Fargo asked, but got no answer.

Ragsdale strode to the body and kicked Maxwell in the ear. "Lord, that felt good. One down, one to go. First, though, I have to find Virginia. I know I left her right about here. Have you seen her?"

The redhead's body was on the north side of the boulder, past Fargo. Lowering the Colt, he revealed, "She's dead."

Unbridled fury contorted the rancher's face. His massive left hand clenched and the veins on his bull neck stood out.

"Who?" he growled. "Who killed my baby? I'll make the son of a bitch wish he'd never been born!"

"A bandit did it. I took care of him."

Like a mighty oak shaking in a fierce wind, Ragsdale shook from the intensity of his emotions. "I'm obliged. So I won't even ask about what happened between Jennifer and you. But I wasn't born yesterday. Get on your horse and ride off. I never want to see your face around Socorro again." He went to leave.

Fargo deliberately blocked the bigger man's path. "There's something I have to know first. You mentioned one down, one to go. What did you mean by that?"

"Not that it's any of your business, but I aim to finish this proper. I saw that greaser bawling over his worthless son." Ragsdale squared those broad shoulders of his. "I'm about to put him out of his misery."

"Over my dead body."

"However you want it," William Ragsdale said, and snapped off a shot. In his haste, he missed.

There were only two unspent cartridges in Fargo's Colt. He had to make both of them count, and he did. At the first blast, the rancher tottered, his left eye gone. At the second, Ragsdale flung his brawny arms wide, took a single lumbering step, and keeled over on top of Santiago Maxwell.

For a few moments Fargo stared at the bodies. "Now that's what I call justice," he said to himself. Reloading, he walked around the boulder into the bright sunlight. Hernando Rivera was running toward him.

"I heard many shots, my friend. Are you all right? What happened back there?"

"Nothing. Nothing at all." So saying, Skye Fargo went to get Jennifer Ragsdale. He would see her safely home, then at long last head for Las Cruces.

The ride would do him good.

LOOKING FORWARD!
The following is the opening
section from the next novel in the exciting
Trailsman series from Signet:

THE TRAILSMAN #170
Utah Uproar

1860, the Unita Mountains—
where greed and hatred made for a fiery mix . . .

Skye Fargo did not expect any trouble. He was winding westward through the rugged Wasatch Range on a well-marked
trail. The afternoon sun blazed bright. Playful sparrows
chirped in nearby trees. Far overhead a red hawk soared. It
was a perfect spring day, the kind that invigorated a man and
made him glad to be alive.

But as the big rider in buckskins reined his fine pinto stallion around a sharp bend, he saw a narrow canyon ahead. He
also saw, high on the rocky canyon rim, a brief, brilliant flash,
just such a flash as would be made by sunlight gleaming off
metal. Fargo went on as if he hadn't noticed. He wasn't worried about being bushwhacked. Not yet, anyway. The range
was too great, even for someone with a rifle. If there was an
ambusher lurking up there, the real danger would come when
he entered the canyon.

Fargo casually switched the reins from his right hand to his
left, then lowered his right arm so that his fingers rested on his
thigh inches from his Colt. He was much too close to Salt
Lake City for the Utes to risk a raid, so whoever was up there
had to be white.

As he neared the stone ramparts Fargo angled to the right so
that he rode in the shadow of the towering wall. Stands of tall

pines and spruce trees dotted the canyon floor. The under-
growth was dense in spots. Scattered thickets offered plenty of
cover. It was an ideal spot for an ambush. Fargo kept on going
anyway. Drawing his Colt, he held it close to his leg, his
thumb resting on the hammer.

No more flashes of light appeared on either rim. Nor did
Fargo detect any movement up high. He halted to listen but
heard no sounds other than the whisper of the wind and the
strident cry of a jay. When he went on, he held the Ovaro to a
slow walk. Minutes went by. Fargo reached the halfway point
and stopped a second time. It was then that he heard a single
dull thud, just such a noise as a horse might make when it fidgeted and stamped a hoof.

About thirty feet beyond, the canyon wound to the northwest. Fargo could not see the stretch which lay past the turn,
but he did not have to see it to know that at least one man on
horseback lurked there. Whoever it was counted on him being
unaware of the fact, and probably figured he would go riding
around the corner as if he were out for a Sunday jaunt. The
hombre was in for a rude surprise.

Cutting to the left, Fargo crossed the trail and quietly picked
his way into the heart of the brush. He then bore to the west
again, careful to avoid twigs and gravel. Spruce trees screened
him as he drew abreast of the bend. Once he passed the stand,
he saw the riders.

There were seven of them. They formed a line across the
trail, blocking it. All seven were dressed in black from head to
toe, except for their shirts, which were all white. Every last
one wore a frock coat swept back to reveal the polished butt of
a six-gun. Four of them were bearded. One, a tall man sporting
a ragged scar high on his left check, occupied the very middle
of the trail. He sat his mount with his shoulders squared and
his pointed chin jutting defiantly at the very air.

That would be the leader, Fargo guessed. He rode on for another twenty yards, slanted back onto the trail, and came up
behind the seven men without making a sound. The first

inkling that they had of his presence was the distinct metallic click of the Colt being cocked.

Every last man whirled. A young one on the end clawed at his six-shooter. He was so rattled that his pistol slipped from his fingers as he cleared leather. Frantically, he fumbled with the gun to keep it from dropping.

"No, Thomas!" the tall man in the middle bellowed.

To no avail. The young gunman finally got a firm grip on his hardware and elevated his arm. He must have thought he had all the time in the world because he was as slow as petrified molasses.

Skye Fargo shot him. The Colt boomed and bucked in his hand, the blast echoing off the high walls. Had Fargo wanted to, he could have killed the fool then and there. As it was, without hardly aiming, he shot the young man in the right shoulder instead.

The impact of the slug twisted the gunman around and he toppled from the saddle, crashing onto his back. His revolver went flying. Still conscious, he tried to sit up, but sagged as shock etched his features. A spreading red stain marked his shirt.

For a few seconds the others sat there gawking at the wounded youth. Fargo shifted to cover them. It was well he did. Several of the men in black came to life and stabbed hands at their pistols.

"No! No more gunplay!" the tall man roared. "The next one who disobeys me will be brought up before the bishop!"

The three gunmen about to draw abruptly froze. Fargo covered them anyway until they relaxed and removed their hands from their six-guns. He then trained his Colt on their leader. The man never so much as blinked an eye. Whoever he was, he had nerves of iron. "You have some explaining to do, mister."

A thin smile creased the leader's mouth but it did not touch his dark eyes. He jabbed a finger at Fargo's Colt and replied,

"There is no need for that, stranger. We never intended to do you any harm."

"Oh?" Fargo cocked his head at the youth on the ground.

"You must forgive poor Thomas. At times he is too rash for his own good. It comes from not being old enough to sprout facial hair. With time he will gain wisdom and learn to do as he is told."

Fargo studied the others. Not one showed any hostility. They appeared more curious than spiteful, but to a man they were tensed to bring their guns into play quickly should the need arise.

"Allow me to introduce myself," the leader had gone on. "My name is Zeke Morgan. My friends and I were out hunting when we spotted you from the ridge above us. We thought we would speak with you a moment, so we took a trail down to this spot to await your coming." He paused to emphasize his next statement. "All we want to do is talk."

The man sounded sincere but Fargo was skeptical. He had survived as long as he had on the frontier because he was as adept at reading people as he was at reading cards. And this Zeke Morgan did not impress him as being a sociable sort who would go out of his way just to enjoy a neighborly chat with a passing stranger. There was more to it than that. Much more. "So talk," he responded.

"Might I know your name?"

Fargo told him.

"Well, Mr. Fargo, I'm not sure if you are aware of it, but these are very trying times here in Utah. There is a lot of bad blood between those who settled this territory and outsiders. Many people have died, I'm sad to say, and many more most likely will before all is said and done."

"Get to the point," Fargo directed. The man could talk rings around a tree, he reflected, his gaze raking the others to insure they behaved themselves.

Zeke Morgan frowned. "Very well. I'll be blunt. We would like to know your intentions. Are you passing through Utah or do you intend to stay? If so, for how long? And where will you be staying? Salt Lake City or elsewhere?"

Fargo almost laughed at the man's gall. West of the Mississippi it was considered downright rude for anyone to stick his nose into the affairs of others. "My business is my own," he declared.

Morgan's fake smile returned. "I beg to differ, Mr. Fargo. You see, we have a vested interest in knowing your plans. Utah is our home, and we do not take kindly to having agitators ride in to stir things up any worse than they already are. That is why we take it on ourselves to question those who cross our territory. It's no more than you would do, I'm sure, if your home and all those you cared for were threatened."

"You're Mormons," Fargo said. He had suspected as much. A few years ago a dispute had flared between the followers of Brigham Young and the federal government over the Mormon practice of having more than one wife. It had gotten so bad that federal troops had been called in.

"That we are, sir," Zeke declared proudly. "We are Danites, to be precise."

Morgan made the claim as if it should mean something to Fargo, but it did not. Skye watched closely as two of the men in black dismounted to help Thomas, who had risen to his knees.

"It is our duty to protect our brethren from those who would do us harm," the leader said. "Some call us Destroying Angels. Others say that we are nothing more than packs of ruthless gunmen. But nothing could be further from the truth."

Fargo did not care to sit there the rest of the afternoon listening to Morgan go on and on about the justness of the Mormon cause. Whether they were in the right or not wasn't for him to say. "You can put your mind at ease," he said, holstering his Colt. "I'm only passing through on my way to California."

"That is just as well. Utah is no place for Gentiles." Morgan glanced around to verify that Thomas had been boosted into the saddle. The young man clung to his saddle horn, his face as pale as a bed sheet. "We will bid you good-bye, then, and wish you well on your journey." With a curt nod, he wheeled his horse and trotted off up the canyon, the rest of the Danites falling into place behind him in single file.

Fargo waited until the last of them had gone around the bend before he replaced the spent cartridge in the Colt and went on. He had planned to spend the night in Salt Lake City. But now he wondered if it might be smarter to simply push on. The last thing he wanted was to get caught up in the uproar.

Soon Fargo left the canyon behind. Twilight shrouded the range when he came to a shelf and drew rein. From his vantage point he had a sweeping view of the city and the great basin beyond, which ran westward for as far as the eye could see. To the northwest shimmered the Great Salt Lake. The trail meandered steadily lower. He calculated that it would take him several more hours to reach Salt Lake City.

Suddenly figures materialized far below, a column of riders moving at a trot. Fargo's lake blue eyes narrowed. They wore uniforms, and the man at the head of the column wore a saber. He had half a mind to move off into the trees until they went by. But since that meant he would not reach Salt Lake City until close to midnight, he went on.

Fargo had been on the trail for days. He looked forward to a drink or two and sleeping on a soft bed for a change. Not to mention treating himself to steak and potatoes and cups of hot black coffee. The thought made his stomach growl.

Going on, Fargo made it a point to keep track of the patrol. He did not expect trouble, but he had learned long ago never to take anything for granted. When the officer and the first pair of troopers came over the crest of a rise below him, he unconsciously loosened the Colt in its holster.

A captain was in command. He raised an arm and shouted for the column to halt as Fargo drew near. Dust caked every last soldier from head to toe, and their mounts were sweaty from being pushed long and hard. The men acted relieved that a halt had been called.

Fargo brought the Ovaro to a stop and nodded at the captain, who did not have the decency to acknowledge the greeting. The officer's hair was trimmed short and he had a thin clipped mustache. After removing a gauntlet, he slapped dust from his sleeves while closely studying Fargo.

"Frontiersman, I take it," the man said in the same tone as most people would use to describe a rabid dog. "I'm Captain Andrew Bracket, Army of Utah. We're on routine patrol. I need you to answer a few questions."

Fargo made no comment. The officer's attitude rankled him worse than Zeke Morgan's. Bracket was apparently one of those officers who believed that he had the God-given right to boss everyone around, troopers and civilians alike. By the man's accent, Fargo judged that he was from New England and had not been on the frontier very long.

"We're hunting for cutthroats who call themselves Danites. They travel in small bands and like to wear black. If you have seen any, you will tell me, now."

There was no earthly reason for Skye Fargo to side with Zeke Morgan. He owed the man nothing. By the same token, he disliked being treated as if he had just slithered out from under a rock. Fargo would be damned if he was going to help someone who sat there looking down his nose at him.

"I don't have all day," the captain said impatiently. "Have you seen anyone answering that description or not?"

"I tend to keep to myself," Fargo hedged. "What did these Danites do, anyway?"

Captain Bracket sniffed. "Where have you been living the past year? In a cave?" A sergeant behind him chuckled, and the officer smirked at his own wit. "The Danites are gun-toting Mormons who are defying the government. They resist all our efforts to bring the people of this territory into line. Pilgrims from back in the States are scared off. Wagon trains are harassed. Anyone they see as a troublemaker is sent packing."

Bracket clenched a fist. "But mark my words. The Army will not be mocked. Their time will come."

"I'd best be on the lookout for them, then," Fargo said. "If I see any from here on out, I'll be sure to let the Army know."

"You do that." The officer straightened. "I wish more people were like you. We haven't had a lick of cooperation since we got here. If you ask me, the United States would be better off if it gave the whole damn territory back to Mexico. Let the greasers put up with all the headaches." Touching his hat brim, he rode on, waving an arm to galvanize the patrol into motion.

That made two sterling examples of humanity Fargo had met in one day. He grinned at his good fortune and resumed his trek.

Below the Wasatch Range lay countless irrigated farms, set out as precisely as squares on a checker board. Brawny men were busy plowing, women and children were doing the planting. The trail turned into a wide dirt road rutted with wagon tracks. Fargo passed people in wagons and lone riders. Most shot him wary looks. A few gave him a wide berth, as if he carried the plague.

Presently the buildings of Salt Lake City reared before him. The city had been laid out as neatly as the farms. Broad streets were flanked by clean homes and businesses. Many citizens were abroad even though darkness had descended, and the majority of them gave the newcomer to their city the same look they would give a roving grizzly. Fargo felt about as welcome as a tax collector.

On most of his previous journeys west of the Rockies, the big man had fought shy of Salt Lake City. It wasn't that he held a grudge against the Mormons, as quite a few folks back in the States did. It was the fact that their way of living went against his personal grain. In all that vast city, there wasn't one gambling joint. Nor was there a single dance hall. And except at a few places which catered to travelers, it was impossible to buy a decent drink. In short, all the things which Fargo enjoyed were not to be found. To his way of thinking, he might as well bed down out in the hills as in the city. At least there he'd have the crickets to serenade him.

But not this night. Fargo recollected a certain restaurant where he had stopped once before. It was still there, and only one horse stood at the hitch rail. Dismounting, Fargo stretched, looped the reins around the rail, took his rifle, and ambled inside.

The fragrant aroma of food made Fargo's mouth water. Four tables separated the doorway from a long counter. Seated at one, in the far corner with his back to the wall, was a portly man in a rumpled suit. He paused in the act of ladling soup into his mouth and regarded Fargo with interest. Behind the counter stood a short man in a white apron who glanced up from the newspaper he was reading and gave Fargo the first friendly smile he'd received all day.

"Well, I'll be. A paying customer or I don't know a hungry gleam when I see one." He offered his hand. "Mike Richards, at your service, sir. What will it be?"

Fargo placed the Sharps on the countertop and shook. "The biggest, juiciest steak you've got, with all the trimmings and a pot of your best coffee."

Richards bobbed his double chin. "Coming right up. How would a side basket of butter rolls strike you? Maybe with a jar of jam? And I've got canned peaches for desert. Fresh in from Missouri, they are. They cost a pretty penny but you've never tasted anything so sweet."

Fargo could have sworn his stomach was doing flip-flops in sheer joy. "Bring it on. Bring it all on. The coffee for a starter, and then don't stop until I'm so full I keel over." Spurs jangling, he took the Sharps to the nearest bench and eased down, sighing in relief at being able to relax for the first time all day.

A man on the trail never dared let down his guard, not if he wanted to reach his destination. All it took was a moment's lapse and he would be wolf meat.

Fargo idly glanced toward the corner. The portly customer grinned and gave a little wave. Fargo nodded, then ignored him. He couldn't wait to tear into the food. It was all he had been thinking about the last few miles. He pushed his white hat back on his tousled hair and leaned back to relieve a kink in his lower back. The scrape of a shoe sole told him that he might have been too friendly for his own good.

"Pardon me, sir. Do you mind if I have a word with you?" The portly man stood with his bowler in hand, his thick lips split near to cracking. He took a tentative step. "I don't mean to be a nuisance. If you object, just say so and I'll let you eat in peace."

Fargo hadn't seen that many teeth since the time he visited the Florida swamp country and tangled with an alligator. But at least this gent had manners. "What can I do for you?" he asked.

"I was wondering if perhaps you are at all familiar with this region? I mean, I couldn't help but notice your attire. You have the bearing of a true frontiersman, and I am desperately in need of a competent scout."

The words had gushed out, as if the man were afraid Fargo would tell him to go take a dive off a cliff before he half finished. "You have me pegged right, but I'm not looking for work right now. Fact is, I'm on my way to California." Fargo turned away, thinking that was the end of it. Given the way his luck had gone that day, he should have known better.

"Really? Well, perhaps it will change your mind to know that the party I represent is quite willing to pay a very large sum for the services of the right person," the man said in another rush. "You can virtually name your own price."

Drumming his fingers on the table, Fargo shifted. "I didn't catch your name."

"Oh. Sorry. Where are my manners?" The man donned the green bowler and held out a hand that had the feel of damp bread dough. "Percy Ornbacher, attorney-at-law."

"You're a *lawyer*?" Fargo said. He couldn't help wondering if maybe he had somehow offended the Almighty and was being punished. The next thing he knew, one of his teeth would act up on him and he'd need to go see a dentist. That would just about make the day complete.

Percy appeared not to notice his reaction. "Yes, sir. And I'm here with a party from Philadelphia on very important business. We need someone to take us deep into the Unita Mountains—"

"Hold it right there," Fargo said, holding up a hand. "The Unitas are east of here. I passed them days ago. And I'm not about to backtrack, no matter how much this party of yours is willing to fork over. So do us both a favor and go finish your meal. Someone who can guide you is bound to come along sooner or later."

"I beg to differ, sir." Percy held his ground. "We've been stranded here for over two weeks now, waiting for a person like yourself. The only other scouts we know of are those in the employ of the Army, and the Army needs them for the campaign against the Mormons."

"Why not hire a local?"

Percy took a step nearer, his fleshy face a study in misery. "Don't think we haven't tried, sir. But the Mormons want nothing at all to do with outsiders. Given the current situation, I suppose I can't blame them. But it is making my job deucedly hard."

The restaurant owner came toward them bearing a tray laden with coffee, a basket of rolls, and the jam. Fargo's mouth watered and he was tempted to shoo Ornbacher away. But the way things were going, the man would likely burst into tears. "Why not send word to Cheyenne? You'll have all the scouts you can handle show up inside of a week."

"I didn't think of that," Percy said, blinking. "Still, that's another week, and you're here right now. What would you say to five hundred dollars?"

"What?"

"All right. Make it a thousand."

Only then did Fargo realize just how desperate the lawyer must be. That much money was hard to resist. It was more than most people made in a whole year. But he still balked at the offer. "I'd like to help you. I just can't. Find yourself someone else."

"Is that your absolute final say on the matter?"

Fargo nodded.

"Very well. I'll have to inform the party I work for that we're doomed to spend the rest of our natural lives here, it seems." Pouting, Percy Ornbacher turned to go, then paused, brightening. "Ah. Here she comes now."

Skye Fargo faced front and felt his insides do another flip-flop. Only this time it had nothing to do with food. For just entering the restaurant was one of the loveliest women he had ever set eyes on, with a body so ripe it was a miracle her tight dress didn't pop at the seams. And suddenly he just knew that he was looking at trouble with a capital *T*.

TRINITY STRIKE
BY SUZANN LEDBETTER

From the heart of Ireland comes the irrepressible Megan O'Malley, whose own spirit mirrors that of the untamed frontier. With nothing to her name but fierce determination, Megan defies convention and sets out to strike it rich, taking any job—from elevator operator to camp cook—to get out west and become a prospector. In a few short months, she has her very own stake in the Trinity mine—and the attention of more than a few gun-slinging bandits. But shrewd, unscrupulous enemies are lurking, waiting to steal her land—and any kind of courtship must wait. . . .

from Signet

Prices slightly higher in Canada.   (0-451-18644-3—$5.50)

WHISPERS OF THE RIVER
BY TOM HRON

They came from an Old West no longer wild and free—lured by tales of a fabulous gold strike in Alaska. They found a land of majestic beauty, but one more brutal than hell. Some found wealth beyond their wildest dreams, but most suffered death and despair. With this rush of brawling, lusting, striving humanity, walked Eli Bonnet, a legendary lawman who dealt out justice with his gun . . . and Hannah Twigg, a woman who dared death for love and everything for freedom. A magnificent saga filled with all the pain and glory of the Yukon's golden days. . . .

from SIGNET